The Promise of

Camelon

by

Kim Kacoroski

Cover art illustrations by Kim Kacoroski, Phillipe Velasquez, and Masha Tatarintsev

Visit the author website:
http://kimkacoroski.com

ISBN: 978-1-947036-06-2 (Paperback)

Version 2017.08.04

Book One of Camelon Series

The Promise of Camelon I

Other Books in the Camelon Series

The Dragons of Camelon II

History of the World According to the Druids III

New Beginnings IV

The Kingdom of the Golden Tara V

Bridges of Flight before the American Revolution VI

Testimony VII

Books in the Oblivion Series

Escape from Oblivion I

Beyond Oblivion II

Oblivion's Edge III

Oblivion's Deal IV

Flight from Oblivion V

Books in the Flight Series

Flight from Oblivion I

Eagle's Flight in the American Revolution II

Flight of the Ascendants in the American Revolution III

Choices from the American Revolution IV

Bridges of Flight before the American Revolution V

Testimony VI

Introduction

*The tune references in **The Promise of Camelon** have been chosen to humanize an ideal. Many of the characters have been embedded in romantic notions, which obscures the reality of their circumstances and belittles their undying spirit. This book, though presented as a historical fantasy, serves as the exception.*

Chapter One

The hidden war in the air

Traps us like grains of sand in an hourglass

Lulls us to sleep

And we forget to enjoy the time spent

Tune Reference: *Sandman*

----America

STUMBLING INTO THE icy cavern, the teenage boy took a few steps and collapsed to the ground. Blood spilled from both of his ears onto the white, compacted snow. His chest heaved with labored breaths as the vapor from his exhalation rose over blue lips. Several men and women dashed from behind the crystallized pillars of ice and raced towards him.

Without moving, Sidor quietly watched from his position. He stood behind the sheets of ice that mirrored the green fluorescent lights bouncing off the walls of the cave. Remaining in the shadows, Sidor observed the small crowd hovering over the body to administer immediate aid. The soft glow of their lights provided enough illumination to quickly examine the boy without betraying their exact location. Like being in a house of mirrors, the real image remained hidden among the virtual ones.

Satisfied that the boy received the help he needed, Sidor studied the entrance of the cave for pursuers. The blue hue of the moonlit sky reflected in the snow showed no trace of an intrusive shadow. The landscape outside remained still and motionless. Only those who lived in the cave could pick out the real images from the virtual ones. Years of familiarity acquainted them with the refraction patterns on the walls of their ice castle.

Marcos, the resident doctor, carried the lad back to the maze of ice walls that concealed Sidor's guarded location. He hurried down a side passage as the rest followed. Sidor lingered in the blue shadows for a few more moments before sliding behind another tunnel on the side. Although all tunnels and passages gradually met in the same hall, the way inside the heart of the castle eluded any creature or human who did not possess a certain amount of intact psychology. Only the spiritually strong could find their way through the constant interplay of light and mirrors. Self-mastery was the key that opened the doors of the ice castle. The residents of the ice castle called themselves "People of the Arctos." Arctos served as their word for the strong animal with the vision required to live in the ice. Arctos referred to the bear of the North.

Marcos placed the boy on a limestone table in a cavern. In the heart of the cave the ice walls were replaced with stone. Two years almost to the day when he had last seen the boy, the youth moaned and squirmed. Marcos placed a tiny dried leaf of Arnica on the boy's tongue and watched the boy slowly open his eyes and regain consciousness. He noticed the dried blood on the boy's left forehead and palpated the skull for signs of fracture.

Voices erupted from outside the cavern. A distinct high-pitched woman's voice echoed among the excited rumble of masculine shouts and hushed feminine whispers.

"It's Alwyn!" the woman cried.

"It's Alwyn," echoed the chorus of voices outside the cavern door.

"He ran off from the Serpentines," somebody surmised.

Marcos covered the boy with a soft furry blanket and wandered what to say to the boy's relations and the leaders of the Arctos. Unsure of his findings, he refused to offer his speculations to the others until he saw the ring burns on the boy's wrists. The boy had obviously been held against his will. The truth stirred him to find the right words. "Alwyn needs to rest," Marcos began. "He has a severe head injury and needs some time to recover. Please be quiet," he said as he gently greeted the throng outside the door. Then he added, nodding his soft brown eyes in the direction of the parents', "He's is like a strong little bear who has a big story to tell when he gets around to it. He's fine."

Without waiting for their reaction, Marcos glanced at his assistant, Elgin, and instructed, "Get the boy cleaned up a bit and a change of warm clothes. He can have visitors once he is settled."

Marcos turned towards Sidor, who had just reached the group in the hall. Walking intently down the corridor, he calmly motioned Sidor to join him. Without a moment's hesitation, the two men walked swiftly down the corridor to meet Zofia, the representative on the Leader's Council.

"How is he?" Zofia asked as the two men entered her studio.

"He'll make it," Marcos assured her.

Zofia nodded with the consolation.

"Now I am concerned about our own survival," Marcos interjected. "The boy's return confirms our worst suspicions. We can no longer work with the Serpentine Federation or trust them." Marcos continued, "His escape raises more questions about how they are educating our children. What type of schooling would kill a young healthy boy or prompt him to runaway? He is barely coherent. It will take weeks for him to regain his full consciousness. It is as if they are practicing a deadly sort of mind control. It is severe enough to cause bleeding from the ears as if he had been hammered."

"We got to work fast," Zofia surmised. "I will go to the council and alert them. The Serpentines will kill us now that their secret has been exposed. We can hide in these caves no longer. They will come after us to destroy the evidence and anyone who reminds them of their conscience. They made a deal with the devil and there is no turning back."

"I will contact the Santa Dragons," Marcos answered. He occasionally traded medical information with the Laplanders, known for their abilities in levitation and penchant for flying furry, mammalian dragons that resembled fire-breathing mice with feathery wings.

Marcos left Sidor with Zofia and walked down the corridor and back to his office. A small crystal with seven faces glowed quietly in the corner. Marcos placed one hand on one of the faces, closed his eyes, and focused. A tiny whisper filled his head.

"Marcos, is that you?" a questioned. "It has been awhile since we have heard from you. They told us that the Arctos people were hiding in caves along with their bears. How have you been?"

"Zelda, the situation is far worse than can be imagined and rapidly deteriorating. Zofia is making an emergency trip to the council, but I sense that she won't make it. The children's school has been placed in the hands of the Serpentine Federation, who use the children in their hybrid experiments. They want to create human machines and graft Serpentine beings. A boy escaped, but he is badly injured. We need to get him out of this place to recover his humanity. They zapped him with some sort of powerful laser. Burn marks on both ear lobes."

"We'll be there by dusk," Zelda responded before quickly disconnecting.

Marcos lifted his hand from the face of the crystal and regained his composure in the room. Having sought medical expertise in favor of the political angle, his countenance relaxed. Struck by the gravity of his own words, he took a deep breath and looked at the dirt floor. His thoughts turned to his immediate environment. Detecting something amiss, Marcos carefully studied the ice cave. A corner of the office had started to thaw as a few drops of water clung to the ceiling. He noticed a slight tremor in his right hand, which served as his dominant hand, and heard a slight buzz in his ears.

Racing out of the office, he ran back to the area where he left the boy. Without bothering to conceal his panic this time around, he shouted at Elgin, "Quick, get any mirrors that you can find and tape them over your ears. We have got to get out of here. Prepare the boy for an airlift."

The boy's family looked at the doctor and quickly glanced at the boy, who started to bleed from the ears again. Marcos had already taped some metallic crystals to the boy's ears after taping his own. He tightly blindfolded the boy's eyes and strapped a blanket around him. Then he hurried out of the room with the boy in his arms.

Elgin and the others followed Marcos's lead as best as they could. Then they ran past him to the landing pad in the center of the cave where the hot springs flowed from the depths of the mountains. The ice walls became rocky and steam filled the corridors. There was an opening in the caves where the sky could be seen. Smoke bellowed into the star lit sky above them. A red ribbon bounced off the haze above them and crisscrossed the natural bellows.

Marcos gazed at the red ribbons and recognized the effects of the most powerful laser known on the planet. His assumption had proved correct. The Serpentine Federation wasted no time in zapping out the witnesses to their human experimentation. Then he heard the sound of the familiar bells from the flying reindeers of the Lapland People. Zelda had wasted no time in calling the Santa Dragons of the Lapland. They arrived in three red sleds pulled by reindeers. They had left the Flying dragons at their base to appear less threatening to the children and Serpentines.

Chapter Two

Soldiers like you and me

March on a grand, infinite road

Called Ventura Highway,

Like the song of a seventies band called America

Until the seasons or changing winds free us

From the alligators, lizards,

And other reptiles in the air of perpetual war

Tune Reference: *Ventura Highway*

----America

MARCOS WATCHED THE other members of his cave fall to the ground with bleeding ears as the effects of the laser had penetrated their nervous system.

"You just have to believe," the thoughts of the Laplanders echoed in the sky. As the masters of levitation, even their animals could fly. They tethered their homes to the earth so that they wouldn't blow away. People called them the Santa Dragons. They hitched sleds to their flying reindeer so they could land on the ice without braking.

Marcos studied the sky to position his escape through the lasers. He closed his eyes and clutched the child in his arms. They needed to save the children for their civilization's future. The Santa Dragons lifted the man holding the boy into a sleigh and quickly flew away from the mountains.

Within minutes the mountainous range turned into a pile of rubble as the laser not only penetrated the minds of those left behind but the heart of the rock itself.

"The children! The ones held captive at the institute...we must try to save them," Marcos yelled.

Elgin, the driver of the sleigh quickly turned towards the domed buildings where Marcos pointed. He dodged the laser beams and hovered over a window where a throng of children had gathered.

"You must believe in Santa," Marcos roared at the throng, which rapidly increased in numbers as more children gathered near the window. He carefully observed the group to assess their health. There were no boys over the age of twelve. The Serpentines had impregnated all females over the age of twelve. Children that he knew from birth had rapidly aged. Those who should be seven years old appeared to be twelve years old.

The window opened and the Santa Dragons lifted three children from the crowd as reptilian guards arrived and pointed their lasers at the heads of the remaining children. Elgin quickly steered the sleigh away from the danger and dashed past the laser beams into the Northern skies.

"HO! HO! HO!" he echoed into the night. He had made off with ten of the twenty million Arctos. Known for counting his blessings, Elgin considered the rescue of even one survivor a success under the circumstances. The planet needed the gene pool of the bear cult as well as their wisdom. The Arctos remained the best survivors and most adaptable to the rugged northern terrain. For over twelve years, they eluded the Serpentine Federation by hiding in the mountain caves. They befriended the fierce polar bears and lived side by side with them like family. Their betrayal came from a similar tribe to the Serpentine Federation, who wanted to splice into their hardy gene pool.

The Serpentines lacked the ability to recreate themselves.Without the spiritual integrity to reincarnate, they grafted their forms onto other bodies. This graft became more parasitic than spiritual possession.

Elgin led the squadron of three sleds towards the Lapland country. The young handsome leader sported a trim auburn beard and mid-shoulder length hair. His father had a long white beard and waited for their arrival at the base orb, a disc-shaped structure that floated in the air. They kept it tethered to several trees five hundred feet below so that it would remain stationary and not blow away into another region. All the Santa Dragons kept their dwellings in the air, because it made it easier to fly.

The original Santa Dragons had been elves with a height of less than four foot. Fifty years ago, the Serpentine Federation contaminated their water supply to create mutations. About a third of the elves became sterile; another third produced progeny less than two feet tall and were called gnomes; and the last third grew between five and six feet in height and deigned themselves Santas. The gnomes forgot how to levitate and remained under forest cover. The Santas surfed all kinds of objects and animals in the air. Known far and wide for their ability to fly the original dragons, they developed blue eyes and fur instead of scales. They loved children because they reminded them of themselves, understanding them like no other being on the planet. Most children could think magically and make things happen, which contributed to the Santas's success in the air. The rest of planet Earth just shook their heads in disbelief.

The Serpentine Federation cloned a Lapland dragon to suit their own race and produce a scaled reptile that flew with webbed wings. Their cloned dragon wasn't pretty but neither were the Serpentines. This reptilian dragon reproduced by laying eggs, whereas the Santa Dragon birthed their young like mammals, hiding their young in pouches like the present day kangaroo.

Marcos handed the unconscious boy to Elgin's father, who took him inside the silver orb to rest. Then he examined the three children who had levitated from the lab. There were two boys and one girl. The girl had begun sobbing uncontrollably in the back of the sleigh. The older boy had fallen unconscious while the younger boy peered wide-eyed at his new surroundings. Elgin obtained the assistance of another Santas on the landing, and they carried the older unconscious boy inside. Meanwhile, Marcos assisted the crying girl out of the sled with the help of the wide-eyed boy.

"Do you know this little girl?" Marcos asked the small boy, who appeared about seven years old.

"Oh yes, she's my cousin. We often play together," the boy told him.

"What's your name?" Marcos asked, checking the boy's sense of orientation as well as becoming acquainted with the lad.

"Devin," the boy responded.

"Do you know where you are?" Marcos asked.

"We are in the Lapland of the Santas," Devin replied. "My cousin told me about them. She said that if we believe then they would come."

Marcos glanced at the girl, who had quieted her tears to listen to her cousin. "How did you know that the Santas would come?" Marcos probed as he shook his head, wondering how this girl knew about the rescue.

"Oh, I heard..." she insisted tossing her wet blonde locks of hair behind her. She shook her head to avoid any further questions.

Marcos took a step back and inhaled a deep breath of air. Somehow this nine-year old girl had managed to tap into the Santas communication network. He probed the blue stillness of her eyes for signs of cognition as he shortened his stature to the level of her head. After a few moments he rose with his answer.

"We need to examine this child under the violet light. I think the Serpentines tampered with her visual cortex. We should check them all for signs of hybridization experiments. Where are your closest medical facilities?"

Shortly after Marcos had proposed his intentions, a woman with auburn hair appeared at his side on the platform. She had been surfing through the clouds on a small wooden plank and quickly jumped off the board as she swerved next to Marcos.

"Zelda!" he exclaimed. "How wonderful to see you! Where can we take these children for examination? I suspect that the Serpentines may have left some implants."

"Quick, come join me in the emergency office. We have a violet light there," she answered. "I have been following your thought frequencies and came as fast as I could. How good to see you again!"

Zelda wiped a few tears from her eyes as she placed one arm around Marcos in a quick affectionate hug and pulled the girl towards her with the other arm. With quick wave, she rushed them inside the saucer shaped house into a small room at the far end of the main foyer. Once inside the room she closed the door behind her and waved her hand over a crystal globe. The wave of her hand stirred a violet flame inside the globe that lit the entire room. A red light beamed from the girl's eyes.

"Yes, it does appear that the Serpentines inserted their lateral geniculate nucleus," Marcos observed.

Zelda moved a clear glass plate to the side of the girl's head. She waved her hand back and forth as if she was air bushing an image. An image of the girl's brain came into view with the optical system highlighted in blue.

"It does not appear that the lateral geniculate nucleus is connected to her superior colliculus," she commented. Then she moved a green lens over the glass plate and elaborated, "It seems that their patient rejected the visual stimulus from the retina, which uses the lateral geniculate nucleus from the Serpentines. As a result, information from the pineal gland became a priority. This would make her more sensitive to visualizations emanating from specific electromagnetic frequencies. She picked up our communication network because her mind naturally sought a higher ordered system and had no place left to go."

"Do you think that the Serpentines noticed her abilities?" Marcos questioned.

"Probably not, but they will be able to connect with her because of the implant."

"Can they trace her location?"

"No, but they could harm her with energy projections."

Although she remained cooperative during the investigation, the small girl began to cry as if the attention to her cranium triggered a memory that still frightened her. The physicians quickly removed the lenses and glass plates from her head. Marcos wrapped his arms around her as she sobbed. Meanwhile Zelda quickly examined the girl's cousin with the glass plate and lenses. She found no evidence that he had been altered in an experiment.

The door to the room opened and Elgin cautiously peered into the room. "What do we have here?" he inquired as he scooped the little girl into his arms, while Marcos went to retrieve Alwyn, the boy that he had carried to safety across the skies. Elgin ushered the girl's cousin outside the room as Zelda made preparations to examine Alwyn in the room next.

Marcos returned and placed Alwyn on a small bed at the end of the room. Zelda waved her hand over the crystal globe, which had gradually faded out after the last recent exam. The violet light filled the room again. Alwyn groaned and rolled his head side to side as he began to regain consciousness under the stimulus of the violet hue. A red beam emanated from his ear lobes and mouth. Zelda quickly began her diagnosis with the glass plate and lens.

"They tampered with his brain stem," Zelda commented before hurriedly adding, "and his location can be traced."

"We've got to move him, before they come here."

"This is a hybrid that the Serpentines will want to retrieve. They will stop at nothing to get him."

"Time to move," Marcos encouraged. He quickly wrapped his patient up again in blankets before carrying Alwyn outside the room. "Elgin, I must get this boy back on the ground."

Elgin instantly summoned his commandeer, slight dark haired man with haunting green eyes named Nolwenn. The commander led them back to the landing platform and summoned his furry green dragon with a soft wheeze. The two men climbed on the dragon's back as they sandwiched Alwyn between them. The furry green dragon exhaled a red flame or two before spreading its hug feathery wings in the air. Marcos hoped that the boy would not regain consciousness while they were airborne. The shock of seeing the furry creature might capsize both of them.

The Furry dragon zoomed through the sky and headed for small clearing in the forest. Marcos dismounted and Nolwenn handed the boy to the man on the ground. Marcos quickly fled for the cover of trees a few feet away. Nolwenn cooed to the dragon and they flew away.

Having come this far, Marcos contemplated his next move as he sat underneath a tree and inventoried his resources. While he pondered a solution, a gnome appeared from the other side of the trunk.

"You have something the Serpentines want," the gnome observed, rubbing his hands together with delight. He relished the notion of troubling the parties responsible for his permanent shortness.

Marcos blinked with the realization that he had inadvertently come to the right place.

Alwyn stirred and his eyes fluttered. The flight had pushed him deeper and deeper into unconsciousness. Now that he was on the ground, his health became more stable, possibly a positive side affect of the reptilian brain implant.

"You're from the Arctos," the gnome remarked with a thoughtful nod.

"Yes, Serpentines wiped out our civilization yesterday," Marcos answered curtly. "We are the survivors."

"And the boy?" the gnome quizzed Marcos further.

Marcos quieted a few moments to reflect before allowing the gnome to join his peril. Then again, he pondered, *if you can't trust a gnome who can you trust?* He sighed and relaxed into the great tree supporting him, before explaining, "He is an escapee from the Serpentine experiments. He was an unwilling participant."

"Any implants?" the gnome quipped as if a foundling came his way everyday.

"Yep."

"Where?" the gnome inquired as he intently peered at the child's head.

"Brainstem," Marcos quickly answered, as if wondering about the gnome's position on cultural takeovers after having personally suffered a height deficit from the last one.

"Well, I'll tell you what. We have nothing to lose," the gnome observed. "The Serpentines will go after any experiment that survives more than a day. It means that much to 'em. We'd love to have him join us. We do better on the ground unlike the Serpentines, who do better in outerspace. Our free-floating brothers and sisters won't want to have anything to do with Arctos survivors."

"I know," Marcos answered ruefully. "You are my best option at this point. I can help you turn this adversity into opportunity. I have a personal request, though."

The gnome silently nodded encouragement as Marcos continued, "I want to go back and look for any Arctos who may have survived the laser. I had family in another section of the cave. I want to know what happened, maybe take measurements and observe effects to create better protection. Besides, there are a few things I left in my lab that I need..."

The gnome whistled a melodious birdcall and ten gnomes appeared to carry the boy off. All gnomes kept their underbrush encampments secret. They carried the unconscious boy deep into the forest like an army of ants making of with a huge crumb from a picnic.

Glad to be rid of his burden, Marcos stood and waved goodbye to the caravan of gnomes. He slowly began walking towards the snowcapped mountains in the distance. The familiar red hue from the low rising sun beckoned him in his grief-stricken state.

The gnome who had negotiated with Marcos, whispered to one of his shy companions, "I give him a week or two. We have the future generation in our hands now. We can pass our lore to him so that we will not be forgotten. I heard that his name is Alwyn."

Although Elgin had not communicated with the gnome cousin directly, they maintained their connection like radar. Unusual events or circumstances created mental images that found their way into the minds and hearts of the gnomes that lived in the underbrush. The gnomes listened, whereas the Santas cultivated a form of selective hearing, which focused only what supported their free-floating lifestyle. In their state of suppressed grief and shock, they clung to their culture as if they could never and would never know any other. In other words, adaptation proved not their style and change never came easily. The gnomes knew this and became known for their wily ways, almost to the point of being considered practically criminal.

Elgin's gnome cousin was called Herlon. He followed his companions into the forest with a skip. Elgin did not know of the missing child dumped in his cousin's care. His loss became Herlon's gain, assured that Elgin and his Santas would keep peace in the skies even if it cost his life.

They gently placed the boy in a small clearing in the underbrush. One gnome rubbed reflex points on Alwyn's feet, another gnome put a red crystal over his brainstem, and other gnomes began brewing a tea to restore consciousness and health. A flurry of gnomes began designing a small stone cottage for his new home. A crew of gnomes grabbed their pick axes and headed for some mines a half mile away. Generally, the gnomes were a cheerful, diligent bunch and understood the magic of singing as they worked. In fact, the gnomes knew a lot about magic, which they had invented to recreate their lives after having been stunted. In this way, they seriously continued the free-floating, flamboyant nature of their past, while keeping their feet on the ground literally.

Alwyn's eyes fluttered and the group of gnomes quickly withdrew. Within a few minutes, he opened his eyes and stared at the gathering of small size people around him. Then he stared up at the sky with a sigh. "Why me?"

Herlon stepped forward, interrupting the boy's thoughts before he became too comfortable with his negativity. "You're lucky," he insisted.

Alwyn turned towards him and studied the small man beside him.

"You are alive," Herlon simply stated. "Others are not."

Alwyn turned away from the man and noticed the red hue in the sky to the far west. He sat up from his resting position and shook his head, while appreciating the few words offered by the gnome. Herlon's comments balanced his growing shock and helped him maintain his perspective, having believed that he would never live to see his family again. Accepting the certainty that he would never see them again, he expressed surprise that he had somehow survived and fell back on the ground behind him.

"Quick," Herlon softly pleaded. "We need to get to our mines. The Serpentine Federation will try to track you. The minerals in the mines will block their radar detection system."

Alwyn rubbed his head as if erasing his past connection with the Serpentines. Suspecting that they had given him an implant, his demeanor became grim when the gnome's words confirmed his worse fears. Nodding at the gnome, he hurriedly rose from the ground. Other gnomes in the group had already started down the path through the brush. He lifted Herlon to his shoulders and followed the scurry of gnomes heading towards the mines.

Chapter Three

Like the sixties in America
Subtle battle lines arose
By the defensive reactions
Of an establishment
Who suddenly changed the rules
For their children

Tune Reference: *For What It's Worth*
----Buffalo Springfield

MARCOS WANDERED TOWARDS the red hue in the sky for forty weeks. He never noticed the black cloud that had enveloped the forests behind him, which had formed two weeks into his journey. He kept looking forward. Instinct directed him towards the region south of present-day Siberia, where the healers for the Arctos had congregated in the high mountain caves. They had a greater chance of survival than those who dwelt in the ice caves. Unlike the ice caves, the mineral content of the mountainous region could potentially deflect the laser-like radio waves transmitted by the Serpentine Federation. The minerals in the rock could act like a giant mirror protecting the inhabitants in a bubble.

Landon, an Arctos refugee from Atlantis, had led a group of health professionals to these mountains shortly before the Great Cataclysm. The Great Cataclysm resulted in the fragmentation of Gondwanaland after a few

"Most perished when the Serpentines attacked. Somehow they penetrated their communications network, dislodging the Santa's two machines."

"I saw the machines when we examined the children for implants," Marcos commented with a nod. Then he quieted and waited for Landon to continue.

"The machines use crystals to operated a waveguide that encompasses the entire planet. It creates an ionosphere that transmits only an alpha or eight hertz frequency," Landon elaborated. "The Serpentines disrupted their silent communication network with hideous nightmares unique to individual psyches. Somehow they tapped into personal histories and exploited them until the subject reached a mental breaking point. The waveguide still stands but many Santas lost their ability to levitate. The survivors now exist in another dimension, which eludes the Serpentines. The Serpentines don't have a spirit and can't follow their prey into other dimensions."

Marcos shook his head at the thought of the catastrophe. "A black cloud followed me on my search," he surmised. "I never looked back, though I sensed the devastation."

"We saw it in the distance," Landon added. "It never reached the high mountains. We can still reach the survivors through the waveguide, but you have to go to a different harmonic. We figured it out and tracked the exodus."

Landon paused as Marcos's niece entered the cavern from an adjacent tunnel. She slid behind Marcos and warmly hugged his neck while he remained sitting on the pillow. Tears filled Marcos's eyes as he recognized her embrace.

"There's my dear. How are you Lorna?" he softly asked as he turned toward her and cradled her face in his brown hands.

She allowed him to gaze at her face for only a few moments before she shyly hid in an embrace again. "I am so happy that you are here," Lorna said, almost sobbing.

Marcos held her and softly smiled. The warm embrace of a surviving loved one soothed his soul. His niece sat down on the pillows beside him and remained quiet for a few moments. Landon stared at the reunion, as he had found only a few things to celebrate since the disaster, and he valued these tender happenings. The threesome talked into the night, reluctant to leave each other even to sleep. The loneliness of separation seemed too severe, creating divides like invisible walls of personal grief. Eventually, they dozed off and awoke refreshed in the same pile of blankets and pillows around each other.

Later in the week, a young blonde man joined them. He had been away gathering food supplies and information among the collection of surviving Arctos in the high mountains. The threesome met the clean-shaven man at the entrance of the cave.

"Marcos, this is my life partner, Ordan," his niece announced.

"Oh what a pleasant surprise! Another family member!" Marcos beamed as he gave the young man a hearty hug.

"Oh there is more," Landon said with a slight chuckle. "Ordan is my son. That makes me a relation. I wanted to break it to you gently."

Marcos laughed as he gave Landon big hug, forgetting any previous formalities. "Well, let's sit down. Tell me more.'

"There's a story that is going around the caves like lightning," Ordan began. "The Serpentine Federation seems desperate now that their power base is gone. When the insurgents destroyed the crystal, the Serpentines lost their connection to the Gauds, who energized them. This is the reason for the hybrid experiments with our children. They must graft onto souls because they lack the ability to recreate themselves."

Marcos and Landon shuddered. Lorna gasped.

Ordan continued, "Some of the cave inhabitants saw their faces while they were patrolling the caves at night. After the crystals were destroyed, the physical features of the Atlanteans began to degrade. Some grew scales while others developed reptile heads. Many developed fangs."

Lorna nodded as she began to understand the implications of her partner's news. She had heard the stories from the survivors of the Santas. Even the dragons of the Serpentines had become reptile-like. Some of the Serpentines had sucked the blood out of the dying Santas. Reportedly this prolonged the life of the Serpentine. Some of the bodies of the female children had been retrieved from the labs. Those of childbearing age had been impregnated and carried a reptile-like fetus, which had died along with the mother from the deadly laser wave. Being in a rush, the Serpentines never finished destroying evidence of their experiments.

"They have no spirit. They have no soul," Ordan continued. "They are only shadows of their former Atlantean selves."

"They have red eyes that sometimes glow in the night," Lorna added, dazed by the remembrance.

"What?" Marcos questioned.

"I heard it from the reports. They have no soul and so there is nothing to reflect the light. The eyes are the mirror of the soul," Lorna responded.

"They shrivel up when a mirror is held in front of them. They can't handle their own reflection," Ordan explained.

"They don't like the light either," Lorna continued. "The survivors noticed that the Serpentines only attacked in the night or on cloudy days. They retreated on sunny days."

"So much for technology," Ordan observed. "Atltantis's technology never sought balanced with spirituality. The Serpentines lack the ability to incarnate or go to another dimension. They could not follow the surviving Santas into another dimension or even transcend." Pausing for a moment, he took a deep breath as he stared at the ground. "The Lemurians call them vampires. Nothing of Atlantis remains."

"The Gauds must not be happy," Landon remarked to lighten the mood.

Just as he uttered those words, a visitor appeared at the entrance to the cave. A soft white light surrounded the young, brown-haired man. He wore a white tunic with a gold sash and clean white pants with copper leather boots. Everyone rose from the pillows on the ground and went to meet him. He raised his hand in the air to signal that he had come in peace. "Call me Emaile," he said.

"Are you sure that it is not angel?" Lorna questioned.

"He's a Light Being," Landon answered for the visitor. "They occasionally come through these parts."

"Thank you," the man asserted. "I am not an angel."

"We never had any of these visitors come to our caves," Marcos stated with a puzzled expression on his face.

"The Serpentine Federation flies around your cave. We prefer to avoid direct conflict. You know, orchestrate things behind the scenes where you least expect it...We're more effective promoting positive steps forward rather than engaging negativity."

"So what's the news, Emaile?" Landon asked, getting to the point.

"Not all Gauds are angry."

"Oh," Marcos responded, seeming a bit bewildered.

"In fact, we are joining the earthlings, the first pilgrims on the planet, in retaliating against the Serpentine Federation. If you see the lights of any flying ships in the sky, it is us," Emaile told them.

"Got it," Ordan said, after having remained silent during introductions. "We are in for one big intergalactic war."

"Yep," Emaile agreed. "The Serpentine Federation has joined with the Black Dog galaxy to build pyramids all over the globe to help direct their spacecraft. Those, who lack spirit, try to achieve the same results with technology. I think they plan to point all the pyramids at Sirius, you know the Dog Star, if not the eye in the sky itself, to resurrect Atlantis and restore the crystal matrix."

"I wonder how many human sacrifices they will need to sustain themselves..." Landon speculated in a rhetorical tone.

"They will take it out of the hide of someone. We must push these spiritual predators away," Lorna proposed.

"Got it," Emaile affirmed with a nod. "Gotta run. Busy with a stellar war now."

Emaile waved them off quickly and left the entrance of the cave. Without a further word, the group watched him walk off into the sunset.

Chapter Four

Some consider god

A nebulous concept

Often measured by the distance felt

Tune Reference: *Counting Blue Cars*

----Dishwalla

AFTER EMAILE DISAPPEARED into the sunset, the group went back to their nest of pillows and stared at each other. A group of neighboring cave dwellers interrupted their gaze.

"Hey there, everyone!" a woman greeted, breaking the silence. She brought a pot of thick soup and placed it in front of them. "We heard that you had company."

Looking up from his seated position, Landon inquired, "Did a man in white pass you a few moments ago?"

"Oh, Emaile, yes. He walked off into the sunset," she replied nonchalantly as she removed the lid of the pot and fanned the aroma.

"Party time," one of the men accompanying her announced.

"Welcome," the woman said to Marcos.

"Carla," Lorna addressed her. "This is my Uncle Marcos. He worked as a doctor in the northern cave. The Santa Dragons airlifted him, and he found his way back home to safety."

"Good Gaud," another woman commented from the welcoming party.

"There are a few," Landon observed dryly.

"That's just it," Lorna interjected after a moment's reflection. "Remember, the Atlanteans were composed of three races. First came the Light Beings, the original race. Then the pilgrims arrived, representing the first Light Beings sent to care for the planet. Later they became known as earthlings. The third group comprised the Serpentine Federation, the ones who lost their souls to technology."

"What's the difference between an illumined one and a Light Being?" another man from the welcoming party asked.

"It is the same difference between the Light and the Dark," Ordan responded. "Lucifer, also known as the illumined one, is the Gaud who went to the dark side."

"Then there are those Gauds who overindulged their egos such as Zeus and his organization," Lorna added.

"Got it," the woman acknowledged with a laugh and began pouring soup into bowls.

The celebration lasted into the night. For the first time in a long time, Marcos felt a flicker of happiness begin to take root within his soul again. Those who had passed would return in one way or another.

The next morning Ordan and Lorna announced their plans to move into a cave they had found to the west. They wanted Landon to help them inspect and protect it.

"If this is the beginning of an intergalactic war, then I want to keep it protected from the Blues and the Grays," Ordan stated. "These various shades between the Light and the Dark are troublesome."

"They slip in through portals," Landon reminded him. "Just make sure that you aren't on one. The Grays stink. You'll know their portal once you smell it."

Marcos came along at Landon's invitation to check out the cave.

"I am considering taking a trip to the gnomes and checking on my patient with the implant," he mentioned to Landon. "I am sure they would love to hear about the remaining Arctos and prepare for intergalactic warfare."

"That's a great idea," Landon encouraged. "The best time to go is when the snow level thaws to the height of that lower cliff." He beckoned Marcos to the view outside of the cave and pointed at the lower cliff. Marcos nodded and understood that he would have three months to prepare for the journey.

When the snow level dropped in elevation, Marcos kissed his loved ones good-bye and followed the route that Landon had suggested around the eastern peaks. He could still see the remaining dark plume in the sky marking the site where the Santas had once lived. Instead of going directly into the lingering gray clouds, Marcos ventured into the forest where he had left Alwyn. Within a mile inside a forest, he spied a small gnome sitting casually on a log under a plump fir tree.

"Hey there!" the gnome greeted. "What took you so long?"

"What ever made you think that I'd come back?" Shaking in head in disbelief, he laughed at the gnome. These wily gnomes lacked a sense of humor, and their lack of perspective amused Marcos. He didn't bother to explain, because laughter came easier.

"The boy eats a lot," the gnome commented, ignoring the question.

"He's a teenager," Marcos stated, growing more aware of gnome's lack of perspective.

"He does the work of twelve gnomes in the mine," the gnome observed. "So he is really worth his weight in gold. Plus he is getting taller and taller." The gnome jumped down form the log and led Marcos towards a little cottage in the middle of the woods.

"Has he had any contact with the surviving Santas?" Marcos asked.

"No, he has been keeping himself busy to take his mind off things. He hasn't expressed an interest."

"How's Herlon doing with the tragedy?" Marcos inquired.

"He anticipated it," the gnome replied with a shrug. "His cousin Elgin fights better in a dungeon than when he is in a downward spiral. He always lost his perspective in a spiral. Somehow the Serpentines knew this. Elgin always flunked downward spiral pullouts."

"Oh," Marcos acknowledged with a sigh. He lowered his head before entering the small cottage. Glancing at the surroundings, he searched for Herlon.

"Care for some sweets?" Herlon offered as he emerged from the kitchen with a plate of pastries.

Marcos helped himself and the other gnome poured cups of herb tea for everyone. "How's the boy?" Marcos asked, after everyone appeared refreshed.

"Oh he's a handful," Herlon mused. "We hope to teach him basic wizardry once the cloud clears. Right now he learning about the various crystals in the mine."

"Is he having fun?" Marcos questioned.

"Well, he makes fun of us," the other gnome complained.

"That should work," Marcos said.

Herlon chuckled.

With a slight smile of satisfaction, Marcos secretly congratulated himself of having achieved the lifelong goal of making a gnome laugh. He thought about the boy's positive effect on the gnome community, including its grieving leader. He found time and children heal all wounds.

"How's the boy doing? Any signs of the Serpentine implant?" Marcos pursued.

"Oh, he has started the wiring the mine for lighting and threatens to bring technology to our humble abode, but we are on to him," the gnome answered.

"Well, at least he keeps himself busy," Marcos observed. "I think I'll stay awhile."

"We have an extra room that just might fit you," the other gnome replied.

"Good, good." Herlon smiled, expressing his delight for the extra hand with the boy.

Marcos stayed eight years with the gnomes until Alwyn matured into a young man. He taught Alwyn medicine and the Arctos culture. Meanwhile Alwyn continued to study the wizardry of the gnomes, who entrusted him with all the wisdom of their life and culture.

"The more you rely on technology, the less you rely on the arts," the gnomes instructed him. "If you are going to do the wizardry of technology, then you must spiritualize it. Remember the lessons of Atlantis. And as for those Serpentines...those who are unable to manifest with spirit must resort to technology. It isn't an ideal situation. Just stay balanced..."

Then one spring day, Marcos said good-bye to Alwyn and the gnomes. He returned to the high caves and lived several hundred years. Alwyn stayed with the gnomes until the last one died five hundred years later. Afterwards, he offered the small cottage and mine to the Santas, who remained in another dimension. Inside the cottage Alwyn left a portal for their eventual return.

Chapter Five

Given the fact that no one is perfect
Some relationships appear destined for conflict
It is only a matter of time

Tune Reference: *Collide*

----Howie Day

ALWYN LEFT THE forest from present-day Wales and headed northwest towards the Norse country. Galactic wars shifted the climate of the earth and the civilization in the high caves fled north. The time had arrived to move on and explore the northern part of the world, which interested him.

He wandered two weeks in the forest until he came to the subalpine region. A village on the edge of the subalpine zone had traded with the gnomes for centuries. Familiar with the encampment by the gnomes' stories, Alwyn sensed that it served as the best place to begin, before engaging the rest of the world outside the gnome kingdom. However by the time he reached the village, he found nothing but the smoldering charred ruins of a recent attack. Puzzled by the sudden destruction, he searched the area for clues to the village's demise. He found no bodies left; only the smoking ashes of the former sod huts remained. Whatever that had struck the village had the power to burn wet grass to cinders.

At the far edge of the destroyed village close to the forest, he spied a pair of small human footprints. He followed the footprints towards the forest and spotted a small rabbit hopping across the brush. The moving bunny represented the only sign of life in the ruins. Moving towards the darting rabbit, he entered knee deep into the thick underbrush. He pursued the rabbit aimlessly for almost fifty yards into the emerging woods. Then he stopped to catch his breath. In the sound of the harsh arctic wind whipping through the trees, he distinctly heard a small whimper. He lost sight of the rabbit immediately. Turning his full attention to the noise, he began tracking the cry as he had once followed the rabbit. Underneath a thicket of thorny berry bushes, he discovered the source of the echo in the wind.

A tiny boy remained huddled in the density of the briars. He did not see the man and continued sobbing. Tears streaked down his wet and muddy cheeks. His eyes remained closed, and it seemed as if the young boy grieved far away in a world of his own.

Alwyn knelt down by the boy's side and gently called to him as he caressed the boy's wet head with his fingers.

"What's your name?" he softly asked, carefully pulling the boy towards him from the mass of tangled, thorny vines.

"Gamaliel," the boy answered once Alwyn cuddled him in his arms.

Alwyn planted a soft kiss on the Gamaliel's head. "Where are your parents?"

"Dead," the boy responded with his eyes still shut. "We lived over there," he pointed blindly in the direction of the closest charred hut.

Alwyn rose from the ground and cloaked the boy in a bundle around his own body. He held the child close to make him feel warm and protected. Glancing at the sky, Alwyn saw the winged reptilian dragons of the Serpentine Federation flying away in the distance.

"They were looking for you," the boy told him with his eyes closed.

Alwyn stopped in his tracks and stared at the boy cradled in his arms. "How do you know?"

"I know," he replied, yawning. Then he snuggled in the confines of Alwyn's cloak and slept.

Bewildered, Alwyn realized that his only experience with small humans had been with gnomes. Small children differed from the senior gnomes that raised him. Sensing that the child needed to sleep for the moment, Alwyn walked back to the woods. The rabbit that he had been pursuing reappeared. The wind shifted and the rabbit changed direction, hopping into the breeze. He turned in the same direction as the rabbit and noticed a traveler wandering across the village ruins towards him. Alwyn waited for the man to catch up with him. Meanwhile the rabbit scampered off in the distance.

"Looks like there is one survivor," the man greeted. He wore a turban and came from another place in time. The man pointed at the bundle in Alwyn's cloak. "The Serpentines mistook him for a rabbit and let him escape."

Alwyn stared dumbfounded at the man. "Where are you from?"

"Oh, I am one of the ten survivors from the high caves. I am a survivor myself."

"Ten must be a lucky number. I am a survivor from group of ten myself."

"I know," the man with the turban responded. His manner reminded Alwyn of the child in his arms. Then he continued, "Some of your relations in the group journeyed to the high caves and told us about you."

"Me!" Alwyn exclaimed, growing more perplexed.

"You are the survivor with the brain implant from the Serpentine Federation."

"Oh yeah, that's me," Alwyn admitted, scuffing up dirt on the frozen ground to conceal his embarrassment.

"It is a crystal," the traveler explained. "That's how they tracked you. You are a walking radio receiver."

"Bummer." Alwyn acknowledged with a sigh. He held the sleeping boy in his arms as he looked up from his scuff marks.

"I have a crystal too," the traveler added. "The difference is that I grew mine on my own through years of meditation and alchemy. So mine is a crystal operated by free choice, whereas yours is a forced situation. You don't have any control over it."

"Bummer," Alwyn repeated with another sigh. "You mean that they destroyed the boy's village in hopes of eliminating me."

"Sorta."

Alwyn sighed at the traveler's words.

"They do not want to eliminate you. They just want you back. You are the only experiment that lived past a year."

"Yeah, another survivor," Alwyn replied in growing angst.

The traveler tried to calm Alwyn down before he woke the child. Alwyn stopped and watched the child stretched a little before nestling further in his arms. He silenced.

"This little one is the key to your survival," the traveler remarked, pointing his cane at Alwyn's scuff marks in the dirt. "Just as you were the key to the gnomes' survival in many ways. They transmitted their wisdom to you."

Alwyn gazed at him. Then it all became clear to him. "This child knows how to shape shift," he observed.

"Yes, he can teach you how to change the direction of your life, which isn't always a bad thing. Building the portal for the Santa Dragons delayed you by a half hour. You missed the ambush on the village by a half hour. You have good karma."

By this time the child stirred in a deep sleep. Alwyn gazed at the peaceful face of the small child who knew his place in life. He relaxed for the first time in his five-hundred-plus-year-old life. Now he could fully understand what he had meant to the gnome community. "You are going to be a little wizard," he cooed at the sleeping child, who silently seemed to smile at him."

Alwyn looked up at the traveler, who had started to step back as if to continue his journey. The wandering wizard holding the small boy shot the traveler a questioning glance.

"The surviving ten from the high caves are time travelers," explained the man with the turban. "That was the secret to our escape. My time is limited here, and I must continue my journey. There is much work to be done. The world is in a tragically different place these days."

Alwyn shot him another look of hopelessness. "Now wait!" he pleaded.

"Follow the rabbit," the traveler advised as he turned and started walking towards the horizon on the tundra.

Alwyn glanced to his left, out of the corner of his eye. The rabbit reappeared from the underbrush and started hopping in a direction back into the forest, except he headed due west. When Alwyn returned his attention on the man with the turban, he saw that the traveler already appeared as a speck on the horizon. He sighed and started following the rabbit. Years of tracking and carrying gnomes had prepared him for this present experience with small creatures. Preferring the small steps that life presented, Alwyn declined pursuing giant leaps of faith and considered his options.

The boy remained sleeping as the bunny hopped through the brush. The lightness in the rabbit's leap encouraged Alwyn and his buoyant steps expressed renewed hope and reassurance. He traveled for several miles before the boy awoke and the rabbit temporarily disappeared in some briars. Gamaliel smiled sweetly at Alwyn when he opened his eyes, having already accepted the loss of his parents. The intensity of the devastation had seared his soul and he seemed deeply appreciated any kindness that came his way. Alwyn lowered him to the ground as he stood on his own two tiny legs. He accepted Alwyn's hand in his, before looking ahead. Then he began walking forward as he inquired, "Where's the bunny?"

Alwyn glanced at the briar patch and the bunny came darting out of a corner as if on cue. "Follow the bunny," he told Alwyn.

Together they journeyed for eight days as the rabbit danced on the path in front of them. When they reached the shore of a huge freshwater lake, the rabbit stopped and sniffed in the air. Alwyn searched for the source of the scent and noticed a small island near the center of the lake. By the time he made out the image of island in the distance, the rabbit had disappeared.

"We need a boat," Gamaliel announced to Alwyn. Tugging lightly on Alwyn's cloak, he turned to his caretaker and asked, "Can you make one?"

Alwyn knelt down and spoke to the boy, "Yes, but you must help me."

"OK," he said before he wondered back into the forest to survey it for supplies.

Being a very skilled craftsman, Alwyn had made many canoes for the gnomes and had paddled them to their various destinations. However, something concerned him about the timing of today's crossing. He sensed that he did not have time to construct a dugout canoe for the boy, and searched the skies for an answer. Suddenly, the boy tugged at his tunic and drew Alwyn's attention to the waters in front of him.

"Look," the boy said excitedly. "There's a man who is half fish that wants to talk to you, Alwyn. He is swimming over to us."

Alwyn glanced in the direction that the boy pointed. A merman approached him.

"Hey there, mate!" the merman greeted. "We've been told of your crossing. Call your Furry dragons and we will run interference. There is no time to waste."

Then Alwyn finally understood. He sent out a thought form of a particular frequency and connected with the same creatures that the gnomes had protected after the collapse of the Santas. Within twenty minutes, Gamaliel began shouting and pointing excitedly in a different direction.

"There's no time to make a dugout canoe today, son," he announced as he picked up the boy in his arms. We are going on a dragon ride."

"Me!" the boy cried gleefully as he eyed the warm, furry, winged, white, blue-eyed animal that had just landed on the beach. Alwyn mounted the angel-like dragon, which had eyes of the same blue color as Gamaliel. He held the boy in his lap as the creature flew to the island twenty miles away. The merman dove in the water and joined a large congregation of people who were also half fish. A giant mist rose from the lake and surrounded the duo on the flying fuzzy dragon. Although there remained zero visibility inside the mist, the dragon and Alwyn sensed the way.

"What's his name?" the boy asked. He petted the soft fur of the flying mammal, which turned slightly to acknowledge the contact.

"Orion," the dragon answered in a frequency that he knew the boy could hear.

"He speaks!" the boy happily related. "He's like my bunny."

"Does Orion has a mind of his own?" the boy asked.

"Oh yes," Alwyn emphatically stated with a nod.

Orion gracefully bowed his furry regal head in response. Gamaliel gulped and eyed the beast with curious respect.

The Furry dragon landed on the island, shrouded in the mist. Alwyn lowered the boy to the ground and then descended from the dragon. He faced the water's edge and pushed the mist off the island through his intention. With the help of the merpeople, he placed a fifteen-mile-wide fog between the continent and the island. The mist rose out of the lake and obscured the island from view to anyone approaching from land, water, or air. The merpeople did not want to be found either, allowing the mist to encompass the entire lake around the island.

Fascinated by the Furry dragon, Gamaliel stroked the animal's head. Orion accepted the attention while continuing to focus on Alwyn. Alwyn walked over to Orion and patted his head along with Gamaliel.

"Bring the others here," he told Orion. Orion understood and looked at the ground as he closed his beautiful blue eyes thoughtfully.

"Let's allow Orion some rest," he told Gamaliel. Then he took the boy's hand and led him into the forest. "We need to make our new home. How about a little cottage...?"

The boy curiously glanced at Alwyn before shaking his head. He refused to leave the Furry dragon.

"Then we'll make a boat," Alwyn promised Gamaliel, who lightened his step at the thought of his new toy. He glanced back at the magnificent creature slumbering on the beach. Orion represented something different than a toy.

Within two weeks, Orion had led the forty remaining Santa dragons to the island. Alwyn constructed thatched coops for them and placed

Gamaliel in charge of the baby dragons. When the babies matured, Alwyn taught Gamaliel how to tend to the nestlings and teach them how to communicate with humans. The boy and man persevered, despite the hard work. In the evenings around the campfire, Alwyn educated Gamaliel on the history of their neighbors, the merpeople.

"They have the same history as the gnomes," Alwyn started. "The original merpeople were the Light Beings that cared for the sea, whereas other Light Beings cared for the land. Remember, the Atlanteans were formed from three races, which were all originally Light Beings. The three races in Atlantis were the Light Beings, masked Serpentines, and earthlings. When the destruction of the crystals removed the mask off the ones who had fallen away from the light, we called them the Serpentine Federation. Shortly before Great Cataclysm, those Atlanteans who had become illuminated instead of being light bodies, stole some of the DNA of the original merpeople. They crossed the DNA with the human form and created the mermen and mermaids that swim around this island. After developing greater lung capacity, they lost their gills. Although, they require saltwater, they can survive in freshwater for short periods of time. Unlike the gnomes, the merpeople remained fertile after the Serpentines' experiments, however, they won't bring their young into freshwater unless it is an extreme emergency."

Usually by this part in the story, Gamaliel had fallen asleep. After a few years, he started to stay awake and interject whatever he had learned from conversations with the merpeople that day. The conversations with the merpeople became the lighter part of his life. Within two months, the Furry dragons began airlifting refugees from global Serpentine attacks. Alwyn transformed the island into a secure base, while Gamaliel learned many things from the different cultures that found safely on the island.

One day, the Furry dragons brought a group of Lemurians to the island. They had a blue-tinted light around their head. Their limbs were long and slender. Like Gamaliel and Orion, the Lemurians also had blue eyes.

"Many Lemurians got along with the Atlanteans," Alwyn explained late one night after the others had retired for the night. "Only the Lemurian underground saw through the mask of the illumined Atlanteans. The Lemurians are just Light Beings, who once inhabited the planet Lemuria or Mu. They were lured to Earth by the masked Atlanteans, whom they failed to recognize as the very same ones who had destroyed their planet Mu. The Lemurians tend to be naive, free-floating philosophers. Most never saw the trap that was waiting for them, only a few. Lemurian insurgents that destroyed the crystals."

Gamaliel listened carefully to Alwyn's evening narrations and eventually Alwyn made one of the Lemurians head of affairs on the island. Well respected by the other inhabitants on the island, the man served as the leader for the Lemurians. The arrangement provided for an easy transition of authority and gave Alwyn time to instruct Gamaliel. Alwyn lived another fifty years on the island. After Alwyn passed away, Gamaliel packed his canoe and said good-bye to the Lemurians, who had amalgamated with the other inhabitants. They took care of the dragons and provided base support for planetary conflicts with the Serpentine and various other shades of the illumined ones. Forming a new society, the inhabitants on the island started referring to themselves as the Druids.

Gamaliel paddled south through the protective mists. When he had gone about thirty miles, a group of merpeople presented him with a small bundle. Lowering the bundle into his canoe and allowing it to drift, he unwrapped the cloth around the warm figure and found a male infant of the human form. The baby cried when he felt the chill of the air on his naked flesh.

"This one was born underwater. He is a merman, but has the full human form. He adapted to life underwater well, but we do not want to test his adaptation skills as he matures. Will you raise him as your own?" merman asked.

Assuming the merman to be the father, Gamaliel covered the infant tightly and nodded his consent. Holding the infant tightly against his chest. he acknowledge his turn to transmit the information of his forebears. "Yes, I'll take him and raise him as my own child," he replied softly. "I'll call him Merilyn, so that he will always remember his family the merpeople.

The group of merpeople submerged beneath the water's surface. The infant stopped crying. Gamaliel wrapped the infant to his chest and turned the canoe around. He placed the infant on the floor of the canoe once the baby fell asleep. Heading back towards the island under the cover of misty darkness, he stowed the canoe in a place where no one else would be able to find it. Then he summoned one of Orion's daughters and flew away with the infant to a remote fjord in the Norse country. In this manner, he kept the existence of baby a secret, especially from the Serpentines.

Meanwhile the merpeople approached the congregation of Druid, refugees, and Dragon flyers on the island. The mermaid mother of the infant brandished a sword above the water and tossed it towards the group standing on the sword. A man emerged from the crowd and caught the sword. His appearance and training set him apart form the others on the beach. Being a samurai from the high caves, he had traveled through time to make the catch.

"This is the sword Calibur, forged for the man or woman who will cut the ties from the darkness threatening this planet. Whoever removes this sword from the rock near the Lake of Avalon will lead the Earth into battle for its freedom," the mermaid promised the collection of people admiring the sword in the samurai's hands.

The samurai wrapped the sword in a red cloth and mounted a Furry dragon. He flew to the stone described by the mermaid and dismounted. A large crowd had already gathered near the stone. People from several castles in the area had arrived at the destination days before the samurai. Their seers had alerted them about an event that would give them hope.

The samurai raised Calibur high in the air and hurled the sword into the stone with the loud cry of a warrior. The sword sank into the stone up to the hilt.

The people in the crowd gasped. They were not familiar with the skill of samurai trained in *chi gung*, where the ability to transmit energy through objects became fundamental. The samurai smiled in satisfaction at his work. Bowing to the crowd with a polite nod, he left the scene quickly and flew the Furry dragon off into the sunset.

The strongest in the crowd rushed to the sword and tried to pull it from the stone. To the dismay of the crowd, it did not budge. Meanwhile, the merpeople appeared in the lake near the stone.

"Take heart and bring this message to your castles. Tell them to prepare for battle. Soldiers from Rome will land in a week's time. Beware the man called Caesar, who wants to take over your land for the fallen Gauds."

The people around the stone rallied and hurried back to their fortresses. Two villages sprung up near the stone within the next forty years as the Romans tried to invade England. With the help of the Druids and merpeople, Caesar had to account for the military failure with his Roman government. This aroused the curiosity of the Romans and they sent settlers.

Chapter Six

Moving through time on dreams and wishes

Becomes empty

Memories of loved ones

Fill the void

Tune Reference: *Time In A Bottle*

----Jim Croce

AFTER MERILYN REACHED the age of twenty years, Gamaliel decided to return to Druid Isle. He left the young man with the Norse people and flew back on a Furry dragon. The merpeople entreated him to care for the rest of the offspring that had mutated to the full human form. The Druids had a burgeoning group of young males with talents that required the guidance of a full-time wizard. Only the males carried the gene for the mutation regarding the human form. The populations of mermen slowly dwindled. The Druids referred to the group of males collectively as Merwyns.

Gamaliel specialized in alchemy. As the galactic war with the Serpentines heightened, he experimented more fervently. The young Merwyns occasionally entered his stone cottage in the morning and found that the master had blown himself up preparing for the day's lesson. Initially it took awhile, but the youngsters eventually learned to track his incarnation amongst the inhabitants on the Druid Isle. He never went too far and would pick up the continuity of the experiment once he had matured and could pour a flask. Word of his experiments reached the surviving people in the high caves and they incorporated it into their culture. They called themselves Tibetans. Meanwhile, Gamaliel became seven times a wizard.

Gamaliel's experimental days ended when a time traveler from the high caves arrived on the Druid Isle one day. This one had a shaved head and wore bright orange robes. His eyes had an unusual slant to them, as if he had been squinting for a thousand years through a blizzard.

"What's the latest?" Gamaliel greeted as the Dragon flyer dismounted, almost tripping over his orange robe."

"Got tea?" he asked with a bow.

Forever the gracious host, Gamaliel bowed in return and then motioned for a Merwyn standing on the beach to brew some herbal concoction. Several merpeople rose from the water to hear the news from the Dragon flyer. Soon it became very quiet around the orange robed man. Only the lapping of the water on the beach could be heard, as rhythmic as the ticking of a pendulum clock, marking time with a steady reliable beat.

"We sensed that there is someone coming to pull the sword from the stone. The birth is imminent. Start looking in a decade. He will carry the will of the Arctos."

A young Merwyn handed the Dragon flyer a cup of tea. He emptied the cup in four long sips then mounted his Furry dragon and flew off into the sunset.

"Well, boys," Gamaliel began, after the Dragon flyer disappeared into the sunset. "We've got our work cut out for us. I suppose the experimental alchemy is over for the moment. Time to start participating in castle life so we can track this new leader."

The Merwyns started mingling with the local folk. Meanwhile Merilyn flew in from the Norse country and held an honorary office in the northeast turret of the castle at Camelon. The largest under construction in the area, the Camelon Castle situated near a rapidly growing village off the coast. Not only did the castle constitute the first line of defense against ambitious Roman ships, it provided easy access for the more congenial types, who preferred trading with the natives rather than destroying them. Eventually, the native populations were infiltrated by landlocked refugees fleeing persecution from the Roman emperor Diocletian. Wandering Roman citizens arrived as missionaries from the different religious factions battling for control of Rome. These people did not fly Furry dragons or possess the knowledge of the earlier immigrants. To avoid complicated explanations, the Druids cloaked the operations on Druid Isle in secret, while the local castles negotiated the hostile Roman settlements.

Constantine also made his way to the region in the guise of a Roman expedition. After being held hostage in Galerius's court, his father Constantius rescued him. Constantius insisted that he needed his son's help with the Briton affairs. To everybody except the government in Rome, it became obvious that Constantine wanted to be emperor to save his life. Apparently he had been in trouble with the Roman government, which often killed family members for political stability. This practice had been initiated by the first emperor, Caesar, when he chased after his former friend, Marc Antony, and his lover, Cleopatra, for political purposes. The natives dubbed the tragedy as a Roman orgy gone wrong. Despite the Roman religion of the time, karma had the final word when Caesar uttered *"Et tu, Brut?"* Nonetheless, brutality literally remained the inspiration for the Roman way of doing business. Constantine practiced an ancient occult religion from ancient Egypt called Mirthism, a derivation of Serpentine Atlantean practices. Although the Serpentine Federation retreated soon after the initial failure of Caesar to conquer Briton, they regrouped and became allies with young Constantine, in the same manner that they used Solomon's Temple once Solomon claimed seven hundred wives and three hundred concubines. Various spiritual practices promoted the existence of the Serpentines on the planet, though the relationship was not absolute. In contrast, the Druids limited their love celebrations to one or two nights a year and blessed the occasion. Rather than build walls such as Hadrian and Antonine, they promoted free exchange between different sects and cultures. Like the emerging Asian cultures, the Druids incorporated balance in their daily lives. They recruited female knights and balanced Merilyn's turret in the northeast with a high priestess in the southwest turret.

Both Caesar and Constantine nourished careers marked by light-filled visions from the sky, rather than silent but continuous lightning streaks by the Thunder People. Caesar had seizures, whereas Constantine linked the vision to military purpose. None of these visions were observed by the men around them, but historians note that the natives never saw Columbus's ships in 1492 until the shamans broke it to them gently. The error came as a result of hero worship of Gauds who traded their egos for the Light. By the time they finished building Camelon, the indigenous population knew that a major paradigm shift separated them from the Romans and they exploited this gap. They attributed the Romans' lack of vision to past life trauma stemming from the intergalactic wars during ancient Egypt, and tried to humor them. Instead of regaining their perspective, the chameleon Romans and their religious clergy only became jealous.

To keep tabs on Constantine's drive as emperor of the hemisphere, many Turks came into the area as well. They knew that they would be next on Constantine's eradication list if Briton fell. Under the rule of a rival Roman co-emperor, they had to play sides without committing to either the Britons or Constantine. Unfortunately, balanced gender relationships proved too much of a culture shock to the Turks. They unwittingly promoted a patriarchal culture due to successful fragmentation by the Serpentines, who had also learned to mess with people's minds as well as their DNA. The Britons knew that they were against Constantine and tolerated the Turk's presence. Not interested in taking over Briton himself, the co-emperor gave the job to the Pendragon or reptilian dragon leader. Unlike the furry beasts ridden by the Dragon flyers, the Pendragon had the aid of reptilian beasts with scales. As unpaid, tortured employees of the Serpentines, the programmed reptiles came to the aid of the Pendragon when needed. Too coarse for humans to ride, the creatures operated on their own, striking down villages with their breath of fire.

Many people across the globe abhorred the idea of Constantine's new world order and journeyed to Camelon to help with the natural, synergistic, ordered world already established there. The coastal castle became a melting pot, assimilating the different nations of the world. One day a dashing Dane named Ryan of Casper flew to the Druid Isle on a brilliant white dragon with sapphire blue eyes. He had a love affair with Ingrod, granddaughter of King Cole, the founder of Camelon. Between raids on Roman soldiers, Ryan relaxed by playing various string instruments as Ingrod sang. Their jam sessions eventually turned into a duet and in time, the duet transformed into a partnership. The relationship birthed two sons; they named the eldest, Ergan, and called the youngest, Arcas. A bear had found his way into the castle during the birth of the youngest son, Arcas. While everyone chased the bear, Ingrod delivered Arcas. He bore the name to honor the ancient Arctos and their relationship with the bear.

When Merilyn relayed the news of Arcas's birth to Gamaliel, the wizard instructed Merilyn to observe the infant. A few years later, Ingrod's talents were required as an ambassador to the Turks. She broke with Ryan and allowed Merilyn to adopt the child and raise him in same manner as Gamaliel taught him. Ryan accompanied Merilyn with the year-old infant to Druid Isle. This enabled him to maintain contact with his son between dragon flights. By the age of four, Arcas tended the dragon nestlings. The mammalian dragons bore their young in a pouch like present-day kangaroos. During battle, they placed their young in a group nest for safety that was either tended by a supervisory dragon or young human. Only the young humans possessed the ability to entrain the dragons and communicate with matching brain waves.

"Daddy, when can I fly the dragon?" Arcas asked Ryan one day.

"Not until you turn five and then we'll go on a ride together," he answered, patting his son's shoulders in loving restraint. "What did you learn from Merilyn today?"

"He taught me how to be like a raven and collect information from all over the world."

"Yes, the ravens and the crows hold the wisdom of the ages." Ryan nodded in satisfaction.

"Gamaliel also showed me his canoe today."

"I remember that canoe," Ryan said softly. "Did he let you take it out on the water?"

"No, but he is letting me play in it and pretend to be in the water. He wants me to use my imagination first. Daddy, what is imagination?" he asked, tugging at his father's leggings.

"Imagination is the dream that you live. Regardless whether it ever becomes real, imagination will teach you many things," Ryan replied as he lifted the little boy to his shoulders and headed for Gamaliel's stone cottage.

"Can I borrow your boat? I want to take Arcas out for a paddle."

"Sure can. Just remember to dry out the inside when you get back," Gamaliel reminded Ryan.

Ryan grinned and took a happy young boy towards the beach for a canoe ride. A few days later, he left for his next mission. Arcas figured out where Gamaliel hid the canoe and took it out himself. He remembered how his father maneuvered the craft and mimicked his techniques, making up what had escaped his notice. He lightly pushed the boat in the water and jumped inside. Then he grabbed a paddle and put an oar in. Allowing the craft to drift a little, he set his sights on a small island downstream.

When he had gone a few hundred yards towards his destination, a mermaid bobbed out of the water to his left. This mermaid had assisted with the placement of the sword in the stone and watched the waterways for contestants. "Where are you going small boy?"

"Downriver," Arcas replied in a voice full of confidence and determination. "What's your name?"

"Oh, you can call me Lady of the Lake. There is a group of us that pass through these currents. We are all on the same wavelength and we support each other like a team."

"Do you have any children?" he asked, hoping that he might find a playmate his age. He spent his days playing with wizards and demanding nestlings. He wanted a change and yearned for an adventure that he could call his own. Though familiar with the merpeople, he had never directly conversed with one. Most people spoke for him or told him what to say. He saw his mother occasionally when he accompanied Merilyn to the Turkish encampments and often cried when he had to leave her.

"I have many girls but most of my boys have the human form. Gamaliel cares for them like he did Merilyn, except for one," she explained.

"What happened with that one?" Arcas asked.

"A wizard with the Sanhedrin caught his father with the baby. He threatened to kill both of them if he did not give him the baby. It was a trap. About three hundred years ago, the Serpentines discovered that there were human forms of the merpeople. A man named Joseph took him and he called the baby Jesse.

"Oh," Arcas said, vaguely recalling the story that Gamaliel told him when Merilyn took him to visit King Pellinor near Arimathea. King Pellinor, as Joseph's great grandson, obsessed over continuing his ancestor's occult work in the region. Though Pellinor possessed an intuitive understanding, he failed to see the big picture. He embarked on an endless quest for a beast, a grail, and couple of other artifacts. Though Arcas never took him seriously, he enjoyed playing chess with this man, who could be so entertaining. He could not figure out how Joseph had managed to extract the twelve districts around Glastonbury from King Avirigas. Rich in lead, the land around Glastonbury fed Joseph who dealt in the metals trading business. Nobody could figure out why Joseph wanted to bring it to Rome.

"I'm going to put it in the drinking water," he often mentioned with a laugh after chess games.

All the locals thought he had been joking. They knew about the poisonous qualities of the substance, the main reason why they tried to get rid of it in alchemy. Though Joseph died before Arcas started playing chess with Pellinor, Merilyn told him this story as part of his pre-game pep talk. Arcas never quite understood what Merilyn meant with this story, which became part of his educational experience. Merilyn always told him as much as he could, as if his days as a helpful wizard were numbered. Arcas sensed this and played the game the best that he could.

Arcas thoughts quickly returned to the Lady in the water. "What happened to him?"

"Well, you know how the adaptations for the merpeople can be touchy. It would be like having a young Merilyn walking around in a desert under Roman occupation with the local populace under the spell of a patriarchal religion. He'd be like a fish out of water. What we feared would happen, happened. He walked around the country and collected a group of insurgents. The Romans felt threatened by the peace and love movement. They nailed seven of them to trees, including three females, and a fourteen-year old boy by the name of John. One of the men named Peter tried to escape, but even the Sanhedrin had turned against them. Knowing Jesse's special talents, they wanted to use him for their own slippery purposes. The governor of the district completely washed his hands of the matter."

"I see," Arcas said thoughtfully. "This what happens when the wrong people are in the wrong place at the wrong time."

"We are all vulnerable," the Lady of the Lake pointed out. "This is why we choose not to transcend into the next life anymore. The Serpentines have tampered with that process too. They turned the entire insurrection into one big resurrection. Who wants to come back with their old wounds?"

Arcas nodded his sandy blond head. "We die so we can truly incarnate, like a natural snake leaving its old skin or a butterfly emerging from a cocoon. Now is the time to leave things behind, especially what is unnecessary. It is like playing chess. When the game is over, it is over."

The Lady of the Lake smiled at the young boy as she did her part in the education of this intrepid young explorer. "Now the game has become cloaked in illusion and poisonous magic. It has a new name and the name is Armageddon. It is an end game for the planet."

"Well, that's a revelation," Arcas observed, commanding a huge vocabulary from experiences with wizened men. Unable to remember where he had heard that term before, he thanked the Lady of the Lake, who obviously suffered from a mild case of empty-nest-syndrome.

The mermaid nodded. She called before submerging below the surface. "Have a happy journey!"

Arcas paddled forward as he thought about his conversation with the mermaind, which prompted him to think on different levels.

Chapter Seven

If the answer is found blowing in the wind
Then there will be no answer
Until the gust settles

Tune Reference: *Blowing In The Wind*

----Bob Dylan

ARCAS BEACHED THE canoe on the nearby island and climbed out to investigate the area. Finding the place lush and uninhabited, he easily spotted an owl landing on tree branch overhead to his right.

"Hi Merilyn," he communicated to the owl. Arcas could recognize the many forms of his guardian, a master shape shifter. Though Merilyn never interfered, he refused to let a small child out of his sight. Ignoring the owl, Arcas continued with his exploration of the island. He crossed tiny streams and tiptoed around ferns. The owl followed close behind but remained in the distance. Mapping every detail in his head, Arcas sat down on a nearby log and rested before embarking in the canoe.

He paddled back to Druid Isle. Returning the canoe underneath the cover of fog, he restored the watercraft to its original position and lightly sponged it dry. Afterwards, he checked on the nestlings, who appeared to be peacefully resting in the confines of their straw pillows. After eating a light supper, Arcas cleaned up and went for a walk on the beach. In the evening he returned to his bunk, located close to the nestlings so they could bond better.

As the years went by, Arcas extended his canoe expeditions further and further down river. The Lady of the Lake became his companion, often swimming alongside the canoe for several miles while they conversed. He loved her kindness and multidimensional view on life. Meanwhile he started learning how to fly the Furry dragons, who also saw him as a friend. He appreciated their thoughtful companionship as they matured together. Nothing seemed to escape their awareness; they seem to perceive his innermost feelings before he sometimes understood them himself. He yearned for the day when he would be old enough to fly his father's elegant white dragon. His father's visits had become less frequent, especially since he had a passionate new lover. His mother, on the other hand, had formalized a new relationship with a man she now despised. Initially attracted by power and prestige, she learned the hard way how much love mattered.

When Arcas reached eight-years old, Merilyn placed him in a school with other young children being groomed as warriors. They held the training in a forest a hundred miles north of Camelon. His older brother lived and studied at another castle about two hundred miles east of Camelon. Arcas seldom saw his brother Ergan, but he admire him greatly and wanted to be as strong and smart as his older brother, who was three years older than him.

Within three months, Arcas formed a close relationship with Maury, a little girl six months older than him. She knew everything about warfare. Maury often ambushed him on his way to school to challenge him in a duel, and he quickly learned to never underestimate women. Bright and very clever, she always did things for herself her own way. Though, she could be very kind at times, Arcas carefully avoided topics that might alter her worldview and arouse her temper. He never mentioned his work with the nestlings, which had been a major portion of his early childhood. He only worked with the nestlings every two weeks now, because his generation of

Furry dragons no longer needed such intensive care. They were older and more self-sufficient. Other children had arrived to care for the newer nestlings and bond with the young dragons.

One day several Dragon flyers landed in front of the school.

"Arcas, what is that?" Maury asked, cautiously sizing up the brilliant creatures as well as the men and women hurriedly dismounted. Watching them, she began to wield her sword.

"Lower your weapon for at least once," Arcas urged in a hushed voice. He strongly suspected Maury had been a Roman soldier in her past life, because she always fought authority figures regardless of the circumstances. In that lifetime, she had probably died trying to overthrow the emperor. "I'll have to explain later. There must be a crisis. The woman leader is my mother, Ingrod."

"What!" Maury exclaimed, trying to make sense of the event.

"Just go with it," Arcas encouraged as he pushed Maury on his mother's dragon. His mom made room for them both and waved for the other Dragon flyers to move on. One of the riders, a ten-year old boy from France named Lancelot won the youngsters' trust with his youthful presence. Even Maury felt encouraged to forget her lack of familiarity with the flying dragons. Arcas recognized some of the other knights from Camelon named Gawain and Humphry.

The envoy rode high above the clouds and headed directly for the mists surrounding the Isle. Out of the corner of his eye, he watched reptilian dragons torch their little hut. Arcas tugged Maury's arm and pointed just before the mists interrupted their view. When they landed on the beach hours later, Merilyn greeted the newcomers and told the youngsters to help Lance board the Furry dragons.

"Who told the Serpentines about the school?" he asked Ingrod.

"It was Morgan Le Fey, King Lot's new wife."

"How did you get wind of it?" Merilyn asked.

"A fairy came and told me," she answered, accepting a cup of herb tea from a Merwyn standing nearby. "The Turks told me that the Roman co-emperor wants to destroy the fairies. His allies are doing the genocide for him. Both the co-emperor and Morgan Le Fey feel threatened by what they call fairy magic. Lot's first wife was a fairy, you know."

"Call it natural synchronicity," Merilyn scoffed. "Magic is for the scientists." Then he sighed and started pacing the beach. "Life in an unbalanced world. What they don't understand, they kill."

"I don't understand why they would let the Serpentines attack the school?" she questioned.

"They know that we are raising an army," Merilyn replied. "This particular army will protect the fairies."

Meanwhile, Arcas showed Maury the bunks next to the nestlings. "Sometimes they climb in bed with you. They love to snuggle, but it depends on their mood. They have a mind of their own."

"I sleep with my cat at home," Maury admitted as she climbed into a bunk under Arcas. Other youngsters, including Lance, found a place to sleep in the hut. One of the nestlings sauntered over to Maury and cuddled under her arm. Arcas smiled, pleased that the nestlings accepted his classmate. Soon all the children were sound asleep after their harrowing experience.

For the next two years, the school operated closer to the Camelon Castle, where the children could easily run inside the stone walls for safety. King Cole had been killed in a conflict near King Pellinor's new castle in the desert. He had been ambushed after visiting Pellinor. His death left the leadership of present day Britain, Ireland, Scotland, and the Isles wide open. Rulers from many sects and kingdoms vied for the recently vacated leadership position. None of the contenders had succeeded in retrieving Calibur from its place in the stone.

Arcas had never seen the sword in the stone and he had no desire to become head king. He just happened to need it on his way to Camelon one day. Though usually very punctual, he had been detained by the mermaid, while paddling up river towards Camelon. Winter break had just ended and he expressed having difficulty pulling it together that day and he missed his merry Grandfather Cole. In his grief, he didn't looking forward to resuming school at the Castle. His grandfather's death seemed so sudden.

Running late, he comforted himself by trying to attain a greater perspective. He commented to the mermaid, "My life usually runs according to synchronicity, and so there must be some sense to this timing."

Paddling the canoe always soothed him, and so he opted for this mode of transportation this day. By the time he could see the castle in view, he looked down at his belongings on the floor of the canoe and realized that he had left his dagger in his bunk at the Isle. Daggers were required this term. To avoid incurring reprimands on the first day of school in his state of mourning, he decided to borrow the sword protruding from the boulder sitting on the far beach ahead. He banked the canoe and jumped out. Scrapping the snow and ice away from the hilt, Arcas estimated its length. Though a little bigger than his dagger, but he shrugged and thought about how he could bluff his way through, making a case for a sword instead of a dagger. Not only possessing debate skills, he handily improvised his way out of difficulties. He preferred coming to school armed as opposed to arriving empty-handed.

Sensing that this sword might be just the thing he needed to today, he helped himself and tugged lightly at the hilt. Arcas listened carefully for sounds of friction so that he would know where to apply the correct amounts of force necessary to extract it from the rock. Like pulling out intact dandelion roots for Merilyn's herbal concoctions, he easily slipped the sword out of the rock as if the metal had been previously greased. Arcas tossed the sword in the canoe and quickly stepped in so that he would not be too late.

When he dropped his bag in the corner of the hut, it rattled and Arcas grew worried that someone would notice that he had a small sword instead of a dagger. Though nobody ever mentioned size requirements, he never fooled his instructors. Instead, he sighed as he prepared himself to play the fool. Tears welled inside his eyes as he remembered his Grandfather Cole and watched the commotion welling inside the classroom. Fortunately, nobody noticed him, because his classmates were too absorbed in displaying their handsome daggers in their sheaths.

By the third hour of school, Kay the White Knight instructed the class to produce their weapons. Everyone put their daggers on the table in front of them, except for Arcas, who placed his big fat sword on the table.

Kay gasped. "Where did you find that?"

"Sitting in a rock on the east bank," Arcas answered as he closed his eyes. Mentally, he rehearsed his lines to avoid an hour lecture on thievery, punctuality, and following directions. Watching Kay's face suddenly pale, he quickly added, "I can put it back during lunchtime and go get my real one. I am just borrowing it. I don't know whom it belongs to. I'm sorry."

"What!" Kay exclaimed, shaking his head in amazed disbelief. "What are you talking about? You are the king over everything now."

"Oh," Arcas responded, still not understanding. "You mean the whole kit and kaboodle? When did this happen?"

"When you pulled Calibur from the stone," Kay told him as he gestured towards the sword.

"You mean this sword has a name?" Arcas questioned him.

Kay nodded and motioned for his assistant to find the other leaders in the Camelon network.

"I need to talk to Merilyn about this,"Arcas protested. "He never told me the story about Calibur the sword."

The whole kit and kaboodle of Briton, Ireland, Scotland, Wales, and the Isles accepted an eight-year old as head king that day. Eventually Merilyn told Arcas the story of Calibur, only after they crowned him.

Chapter Eight

There is profound leadership

In a youthful approach

Tune Reference: *I'll Be There*

----Jackson Five

"MERILYN, WHY DID you not tell me about Calibur sooner? You told me about everything else," Arcas quizzed Merilyn after the crown had been placed on his head.

"You would have steered your little canoe around it," he answered.

"You are right," Arcas replied sharply at the wizened man.

"Sooner or later, we all must grow up. Some sooner than others and that is no fault of mine. It is your fate. Deal," the wizard said. "We always knew that you had that magic touch. The rest of us have to look at ourselves in the mirror and ask why we don't have it. Those who can't do, teach. Talk about a rude awakening in self-development. You made it look easy," Merilyn rambled.

Arcas ignored his complaints. "That's not my fault, but I'll remember the bit about the teaching. OK, so how about running the country?"

"Wing it," the astute magician advised. "Think about it this way: If you can pull a sword out of a rock, then you should be able to pull a rabbit out of a hat. Government is similar."

"Alright, Merilyn, where should I start first?"

"How about my mother, the Lady of the Lake. She is the one who brought Calibur in the first place."

"Great idea. I'll go paddle out there now."

The Lady of the Lake seemed more than happy to give Arcas an earful about how the country should be ruled. With all the advice that she had given him over the years, he recalled every lesson that he had ever learned during his days on the Druid Isle. Then he began implementing them and visiting the leaders of the various kingdoms. People from around the world heard of his earnestness and came to help. Meanwhile, the crowning of the new king caused the enemies to momentarily retreat and regroup.

One of Arcas's first accomplishments included the establishment of a cultural exchange program with the present-day Spain and Portugal region. It took a few years, but eventually a group of three arrived. The woman, Egressa, a dark-skinned redhead, came from the Moors. She filled the office in the southwest turret as Merilyn's counterpart. Besides being very intuitive, her exotic features made her a desirable date at the Druid Fires during autumn. She sported a huge falcon in her company and communicated to the bird with a brilliant red stone in the ring on her left hand. She could reflect the red rock in the sunlight and guide the falcon to any destination.

One of her companions, an Orange knight from Spain, came to help as well as learn new skills. Though he nourished a passion for Egressa, he refused to commit to a relationship. Though Egressa continued her interest in the Orange knight, she sidestepped any commitment. Having too much fun with the relationships that ensued after the Druid fires, she created tension in the dynamics with the Orange knight. This kept their relationship affectionate but edgy. The third member of the traveling trio simply made swords and pretended that he had nothing to do with the dramatic antics of the other two.

Egressa immediately found an apprentice to aid with intelligence operations in the southwest turret. The apprentice named Igraine had a sister named Laticia, who served as a doctor for the local village and Camelon network. The two sisters were very close, young, beautiful, and very bright. Within a year Egressa and Igraine constructed a power vortex within the cylindrical walls of the southwest turret, which amplified the energetic thought forms produced by the Camelon collective. Egressa proved to be wise counsel, and many people sought her company for this reason as well. Even Arcas enjoyed chatting with her over a cup of herb tea, which she concocted from the supplies in her tower. She helped with intelligence operations pertaining to the Camelon network and understood the innermost network.

While Egressa and Igraine ran experiments in superradiance from their power tower, Merilyn and Arcas continued to interview the surrounding countries and provinces. Before his death, Joseph of Arimathea brought a bishop from the new religion that had emerged from the Mideast. Though the man came from Greece, he planted himself in Briton with the title "Bishop of Canterbury." Arcas and Merilyn paid a visit to this province, which had once been the landscape of King Pellinor before he relocated to pursue his recent quest. Many of King Pellinor's sons and daughters remained in the area and provided a congregation for the new clergy.

Unfortunately, finding the bishop out of town when they arrived, they questioned the local authorities.

"Where is he? He knew that we were coming," Merilyn asked the monk who blocked them from entering the church.

"He went to Nicea on an emergency call from the new emperor, Constantine. The bishop did not mention any visitors. May I tell him that you called? What are your names?"

"Tweedle-dum and Tweedle-dee," Merilyn replied, while hurriedly nudging Arcas away from the church. "We just wanted to ask about baptism fees."

"Any news from Nicea?" Arcas asked the monk. Surveying the area, he gathered information about the sudden change in heart from this region.

"Why yes, odd you should ask. Do you read? I've been transcribing scrolls on the Council of Nicea."

"I have friends that read," Arcas lied, pretending to be Tweedle-dum. "May I have one? I like to keep up on the latest news."

Merilyn eyed Arcas and decided to leave the king waiting on the church steps alone.

"Get the dragons ready to fly, Merilyn," Arcas told him in a whisper. "I'll be running right behind you."

When the monk returned with the scroll, Arcas seized it and quickly waved good-bye. He said, "Gotta run. Got a few sheep loose in the pasture."

He met Merilyn in the forest where they had hidden their Furry dragons. They mounted their Furry dragons and flew under the cover of the rising mists. At the castle, Arcas skimmed the scroll before bringing it to the southwest tower for full translation and evaluation.

"It is obvious that the new Bishop of Canterbury values his relationship with Constantinople over Briton. That is perfectly clear. But what is more disturbing is how this new creed targets our own spiritual values. This is a different kind of war," Arcas explained.

Merilyn nodded. "I will relay this information to Gamaliel and the people on the Druid Isle."

Then he left immediately. Merilyn never dallied; he went straight to his mentor with the information. When Gamaliel heard the news, he appeared very grave and tugged at his beard. "This confrontation that is brewing seems rather ominous. The circumstances around King Cole's death remain mysterious. Guess how many people from across the globe have been coming to Camelon to help defend everything we encourage. We have an epidemic. I've been tracking the past lives of those involved and it seems many are survivors from the early Christian movement. Many went to another dimension, and they have a conflict with the emerging new world order. Now this new church is surfacing to finish annihilating their spirit. The survivors are stuck in a pattern due to past trauma. They can be easily manipulated on a psychic level."

"What about me?" Merilyn asked.

"We'll see how long it takes for the Serpentines to use the one they crucified to manipulate the rest." Gamaliel answered. "Meanwhile, keep it light and have as much fun as possible. It is our best psychic defense."

Merrily knew Gamaliel referred to the captured Merwyn infant once in Joseph's custody. He sighed and paced the beach with Gamaliel.

"What about the Camelon Castle?" he pondered out loud.

"Young Arcas still has some time to set things up," Gamaliel observed. "I'll keep watch over it from the base here."

With Gamaliel's reassurance, Merilyn nodded quickly and left the beach. He returned to the castle and met Arcas reclining on a small couch in his northeast turret.

"It is noisy in the southwest turret. People sense that trouble is brewing. I like to come up here and think for myself as I gaze at the stars around the North Pole. The view from here is incredible."

"Well I see that you are on it," Merilyn replied.

"Yep, it is in my face," Arcas quipped.

Chapter Nine

Meandering through the world
The lines of communication
Connect loved ones closer
Over the distance and strain

Tune Reference: *Wichita Lineman*
----Glen Campbell

YEARS PASSED AS Arcas matured and solidified the kingdom. Briton, like other countries at this time in history, consited of a collection of various tribes ruled by chieftains rather than kings. When several tribes came together under a particular leader, the person earned the title "king." For this reason, the Lady of the Lake in all her wisdom, knew that it would literally take someone that could melt stone to break down the barriers between the factions and unite Briton in an empowering manner without interference from the Arabs, who had intermarried into the Hebrew tribes since the days of Abraham. Meanwhile Merilyn and the Merwyns began to show signs of mental deterioration as the Serpentines tapped into their brain waves. One day Merilyn just disappeared without telling anyone of his whereabouts. Arcas decided to check with Egressa, who had a child with Merilyn. The small three-year-old boy toddled behind her in the southwest tower. He had platinum blonde hair and carefully watched everything his mother did.

"Who would have guessed that behind all that gray, Merilyn was a blond?" Arcas laughed after lifting the boy high in a playful greeting. He enjoyed being the godfather for the son of two of his best friends.

"His father, Merilyn, had gold scales and swam near the Norse," Egressa recalled. Her voice drifted off with the memory of her partner.

"Merilyn is gone," Arcas said, interrupting her reflective mood.

"Yes, I know," Egressa rejoined, intimidating the danger for her and the child. Their enemies had succeeded in destroying Merilyn's consciousness and would try to sever all his relationships, especially those closest to him.

"Where do you want to go?" Arcas asked, getting straight to the point.

"Germany," she suggested.

"You can stay with my mother there. She is done with the Turks. There is a Turk in the Camelonvillage that tells me everything I need to know. All I have to do is observe him."

The next morning Arcas paddled Egressa and her child through the mists to a place where Ingrod could meet them. She would fly them to Germany on her dragon, after weeks of making their way through the mists. Now that Merilyn and the Merwyns had disappeared, they hid the merpeople foundlings in Germany. At the designated site in the thick woods, Ingrod sat the little boy in her lap like a satisfied grandparent, and happily waved to Arcas as she took off. Relieved, Egressa strapped herself behind Ingrod on the dragon. She blew a light kiss at Arcas as they departed.

Arcas returned to the castle and secured the turrets. Egressa's assistants led by Igraine took over Intelligence operations. Lance came to help with operations in the Merilyn's former office, seeming to be unaffected by the turbulence of events. Gamaliel reasoned that Lance had developed immunity from trauma in a recent past life as John the Baptist.

The ensuing attack by the local Roman soldiers came within the week. Gamaliel brought Druid reinforcements and saved the castle as well as Arcas's life. Several Romans cornered Arcas and threatened to bludgeon him to death. Gamaliel threw the powdered results of a former alchemy experiment at them and caused an explosion.

"Great job," Arcas told Gamaliel before he teetered over from a blow to his left thigh.

A powerful man as well as a wizard, Gamaliel slung Arcas over his back like a sack of potatoes and headed towards a secret passageway leading to the village on the other side of the castle. Fragments fell all around them as the Romans hurried back to their ships. When Gamaliel had made his way to the village, he located the doctor's hut and knocked on the door.

"I have King Arcas," he announced. "Can you patch him up for me? I have other business to attend."

Laticia, Igraine's sister, opened the door and motioned for Gamaliel to place Arcas in a small bed located in a window alcove. Soon other injured would arrive and demand her services. She operated off her kitchen table and placed patients in various huts and castle rooms for recovery. Seeing Arcas on her doorstep, she immediately decided that she wanted him to stay in her home. She took personal interest in the man that Gamaliel had brought to her and told Gamaliel to leave him on her bed.

Arcas could feel her soft, delicate fingers mend the wound on the side of his leg. Though he had been sutured before, he could not remember a more loving touch. He relaxed and felt a sense of peace permeate his entire body. Laticia told him to stay and not move. So he did and drifted into a deep sleep. He remained a couple of days in her hut and watched the woman work.

When she wasn't mending wounds and tending to patients, she cooked, cleaned, and gardened. Two women came to help her occasionally and kept the hearth warm while she made house calls. Arcas enjoyed observing her, because she seemed happy and full of life. They made easy conversation and never seemed at a lost for words.

After he had recovered, Arcas frequented the doctor's home. Sometimes they took walks in the meadow, and other times they played the lute together. He began staying for dinner; then he began to spend the night. After two years he moved in with her, and they had a beautiful daughter, Joslin.

Laticia's mother had been a Viking, who partnered with a Lemurian on the isle. Arcas's father was the son of the Viking king and a Danish princess named Lady Casper. Though she worked with the white horses near the Caspian Sea, his mother had Ryan while on a diplomatic mission in Denmark. Raised in Denmark, Ryan left when some of the Viking leaders started to intermingle with the Grays. Ingrod told Ryan about the resistance movement at the Druid Isle, and Ryan decided to join. In many ways, he remained a prince without a country and King Cole adopted him for all purposes. His encounter with Ingrod at Camelon had not been the first time they met, though it represented the first time that he had been to Scotland. Several more Vikings joined the collection of people around Druid Isle. Some joined the warrior group and were known as the Red knights. Arcas did not see his father much because he negotiated with a portion of the Vikings linked to the Grays. Though King Cole would have preferred to keep them as allies, he suspected that they would seize Camelon for themselves if Rome failed.

To the east, the new religion flourished and Joseph of Arimathea successfully introduced several relics to the region. The relics made the new religion appear more tangible to the local population. One of the relics known as the Holy Grail had been used by the unfortunate Merwyn at his last meal. Unlike the other cups collected by Joseph, this one possessed special healing powers characteristic of the merpeople. He threw the others away and kept this one, calling it the Holy Grail. During a heated discussion with his great grandson Pellinor, he threw it in a well at Glastonbury.

"What do you mean that you want to resurrect your young dead wife?" he asked Pellinor. "Get over it. What ever happened to the others? They were more your age."

"But she is the only woman who ever loved me," Pellinor claimed.

"That's your problem," Joseph retorted. "Look, don't you see the hoax used to perpetuate the sun god myth from ancient Mithraism. The Arabs from Egypt would just love to plant it in your psyche. It is a foot in the door for the Serpentines. The emperor and his mother are fond of that archetype because of its success in the pyramid civilizations. They know how to control people through religion. It works like an opiate."

"That's what I need—A hallucinogenic drug!" Pellinor exclaimed. "Look, one of my Persian nephews gave me this weed that grows around graveyards. He told me that it could bring life everlasting. I can bring her back if I take this weed."

"Let me see that," Joseph demanded.

Pellinor fished through his pockets and produced the weed that the Persian had given him.

"That's belladonna, you fool," Joseph stated.

"Too late. I already took a dilution. I leave for a quest tomorrow and I'll take the rest on the road."

"You beast! You are the questing beast," Joseph said. "You are leaving your lush estate for the desert."

"You are just being mean," Pellinor remarked. "I need this woman back. I am off on a noble quest. You don't understand."

"You see this Holy Grail..." Joseph interrupted. "You will never find it until you begin to look within."

With those words, Joseph hurled the Holy Grail into the well, which later became know as Chalice Well.

"You are just trying to trick me," Pellinor continued, and he left for his quest.

When Arcas repeated this story that he had heard in the village, Laticia asked him, "Where is the Persian, the one who gave the weed to Pellinor? I'd watch him very carefully."

"He seeks refuge at Camelon," Arcas said with a smile. "I agree that the man is wily; I think his relations want to hang him."

Chapter Ten

It is the consistent, anticipated
Tender touches that keep us alive
And returning home safely

Tune Reference: *Back Home Again*
----John Denver

WITH LATICIA'S ENCOURAGEMENT Arcas journeyed to a small island south of Avalon, the closest Roman settlement. The island was inhabited by a particular race of Light Beings known as Warrior Celestials. Their leader, Morgana, was a lithe woman about ten years older than Arcas. He held a great of respect for Morgana and her rough crowd. They got directly to the point in their dealings between heaven and earth, always taking the galactic road wherever possible and even barely possible. They had entered the earth's dimension during the intergalactic wars in ancient Egypt and had never left. The intergalactic wars had never really ended; they just assumed different forms and went underground. No treaties were ever recognized and so these Warrior celestials played it straight, knowing that there were no rules left to break. Being extremely talented, they brought gifts of science, art, music, and inspiration from the heavens. Their celestial singing particularly irritated the Romans across the lake. The soldiers often forgot their military mission when they heard the sweet music drifting in their ears. Sometimes they would put down their swords and fall asleep. They found it difficult to kill the musicians and singers responsible. Roman operations had been stymied for years by their melodies. The Romans called them the Sirens, whereas everyone else in the region referred to them as the Flower Children.

Arcas paddled his canoe past the Roman encampment and towards the small island with the Flowery Meadows. The Siren songs only distracted those who worked at cross-purposes to the Warrior celestials. Music served as their best offensive weapon. Arcas drifted towards the embankment and beached his canoe. Then he made his way through the knee-high grass to a stone cottage on the hill where he knew he could find Morgana. He found her sitting on a rock in front of her cottage restringing her harp with several friends. She immediately stopped her work when she saw him in front of her. Motioning her friends away for a private conversation with the young man, she got directly to business, "What can I do for you, Brother Sun?"

"I need your help, Sister Moon," Arcas answered. He never minced words when dealing with celestials. "Difficulties are brewing on the mainland."

"What do you want us to do?"

"Keep Pellinor entertained on his endless quest and out of the area."

"Will do," she answered. "Anything else?"

"Can you sidetrack a few Roman ships heading for Camelon?"

"How about stirring up a storm?"

"At least a few, in case they send replacements. Can you catch them in the Mediterranean, before they even see our coastal waters? I wouldn't want them to think that we had anything to do with it. You know, set up a little decoy just like old times."

"We'll do our best," Morgana offered. "Several in our group already came up with the same suggestion. Many have volunteered to go on the expedition next week. We must be on the same wavelength."

"Thanks, Sister Moon," Arcas politely said before departing the island. Although they had no immediate familial ties, Arcas and Morgana had found that they complemented each in many ways as if they formed their own little universe. They also wanted to keep this universe safe and far away from Serpentine fangs.

Arcas hopped in his canoe and paddled past Avalon under the spell of a celestial chorus of about two hundred angels. This time the island band played music that the world would eventually recognize as Beethoven's "Moonlight Sonata." Morgana always wanted to perfect her melodies before future reincarnations. He watched the Romans soldiers swoon and dance lightly in the fragrant air coming from the Flowery Meadows. *Just as life should be*, he thought. Meanwhile he hurried home to his life partner, who waited for him in her small hut in the village.

"How did it go?" Laticia asked as he lifted her in the air with a warm embrace.

"Oh, you know me and heavenly bodies," he answered before passionately kissing her. "I'll never understand astrology like your sister, Igraine. I've always been more like an astronomer. I'd rather gaze at the starlight and track its motion."

She smiled without saying another word. Instead she kissed him. He carried her to the bed in the alcove and they made love through the night. The next morning, Laticia made home visits as Arcas made breakfast and chopped wood. Connie, Laticia's apprentice, had brought over Joslin, their one-year old daughter early in the morning for nursing. Laticia had been very busy with patients until shortly before Arcas arrived. Two women in the village cared for the hearth in Laticia's absence, and helped watch the children. Connie's partner, a Red knight presently away on a mission in

Germany, protected Ingrod's castle. Arcas expected him to return with Egressa and her son soon. The refugees were no longer safe in Germany.

His mother remained at the family castle in Germany. With the dissension arising between the Roman co-emperors themselves, diplomatic relations had been limited. Ingrod had put everything on hold until the bigger players in the world worked things out, which of course, was not going to happen. The co-emperors battled to death, then killed off those who stood between them and world dominion. This operating mode resulted an all-or-nothing proposition for any co-emperor. They could not leave any loose ends; anything not under their control became a potential threat and possible vehicle for another takeover. Rather than choose sides between co-emperors, Ingrod simply backed off. She did not want to choose the losing co-emperor and become a target. Time favored Camelon.

Many people from different sides in the battle for preservation of the planet took refuge in Germany. One's neighbor in Germany might be one's enemy in another country. For this reason, nobody questioned their neighbors in Germany. For sometime Germany became a great place to get lost and hide from world affairs. However, Constantine's move to Constantinople blew the cover on those hiding in Germany. Those hiding in Germany had rapidly become another loose end to take care of. When one's neighbors began disappearing the in the night, the inhabitants entertained an eerie suspicion that they would soon be next.

Not one to take chances, Ingrod reasoned that the safest place right now on the planet was Camelon. Refugees came pouring in from various corners of the globe. Some came to fight and some came to hide. Unfortunately, some of the local estates began aligning with the dominant religion of the new world order. This brought the conflict closer to Camelon. Maury and her two siblings had recently inherited their father's vast kingdom in Briton. She busied herself with her three children and her new role as queen. Though her partner cared for the children during her absence, the demands of being a ruler pressured her to keep the peace with Constantine's bishop in Canterbury. He demanded baptisms for all pagans in the region and Maury's brother and sister had already complied with their kingdoms.

"How about paying a visit to the kingdoms in Briton and see how Maury is getting along?" Laticia asked Arcas one day as he began preparing for his tour of the far countryside.

"Great idea. I've already packed for the excursion and decided to take a horse instead of a dragon. The horse will be less noticeable. Don't want to give the locals culture shock. I know where Maury wanders and I plan to wander there myself today."

Then kissed her softly on the lips as he told her, "Amazing how we both get all these great ideas together. It's like we are making our way in a blizzard, finding ways to connect although we can barely see each other."

Laticia returned his soft kiss, before throwing a few more items in his pack in a more businesslike manner. She patted the horse and waved him off.

Arcas found Maury at her favorite stream where they had often played as children. She thoughtfully reflected at the rushing waters and barely seemed to notice Arcas when he dismounted several yards away.

"No dragons today?" she asked.

"No, I didn't want to make a show. Dragon flying is becoming a lost art in these forests," Arcas said, getting quickly to the point.

Maury didn't dally either. She got straight to the point. "The Bishop of Canterbury wants you to marry my sister, Guinevere. This will formally make her the queen of England."

"I already have a queen that I love," Arcas responded. "Our daughter Joslin is now almost two years old."

"He plans to wage war against those with pagan arrangements."

"Is that Constantine's excuse to destroy Camelon?" Arcas inquired. "He wants to own personal affairs."

Maury did not reply. She rose and glanced quickly at Arcas. Then she stared at the bank of trees across the stream. "You know I have always considered you as a brother."

"Which is why you are not my queen," Arcas said truthfully. "An arranged marriage would only serve to formalize the brother-sister relationship. We were classmates or litter mates," Arcas continued. "The Romans have a habit of arranging relationships, and then in the end they kill each other. Yet they call us infidels. What kind of fidelity is that? To not be true to one's heart and what one loves? I entertain Guinevere as a sister, but mostly because she is your sister. I have chosen the paths of the Light spirits. Your sister partners with the Trojans, and it would be the end of our planet if I complied. Then the Bishop would demand that the king gets baptized, and that would mean spiritual doom for us all. The Serpentines would get a foot in the door to the castle. Nobody would be safe."

"You'll have to battle it out with the bishop and Constantine on your own," Maury told him.

"That will start," Arcas answered before mounting his horse. Before turning away, he reminded her, "Caesar Augustus had his designs on Helen's son, Constantine, when Caesar allowed the Moors to crucify Jesse, the one that the Arabs call Jesus Christ. The Moors were behind Julius's assassination; they are brutes."

On the way back to the village, Arcas paid a visit to his successor and second in command, Tristan the Yellow Knight. Tristan lived on a smaller estate with his partner Eilene the Green Knight and their three children. Eilene told Arcas that Tristan was away dueling with a wicked sorcerer in area. Though, there were several wicked sorcerers in the region, only one sorcerer concerned Tristan, who would probably be dueling with this particular sorcerer until the end of time. They had been dueling with each other for several lifetimes and there seemed to be no end in sight to the conflict.

Arcas left instructions for a stable attendant to return his horse to the castle. He told them that he would be going on another excursion upriver. Arcas quickly left the area and retrieved his canoe from a hiding place in a nearby forest. Then he paddled downriver to Morgana's Flowery Meadows. He didn't want anyone to know where he was going. Ever since the Turks had sacked the castle to haul off the Persian youngster who had given the weed to Pellinor, he became more covert in his relationships. The Greek sorcerers that had advised Alexander the Great had been in league with the Trojans, ancient enemies of Sparta.

Again, Gamaliel had seized him from the jaws of death. Now Arcas looked over his shoulder a little more. By the time the Camelon knights reached the Turkish prisoners, they found the Persian barely alive. Pellinor's associates had brutally raped and tortured him. He died from his wounds a few days later. Laticia had done her best to ease his suffering, and Gamaliel had removed the tracking device from his body, which the "Illumined Ones" had implanted. Gamaliel said that his teacher, Alwyn, had taught him about such implants from the Serpentine Federation. Though he had never found one before in his life, he had learned how to detect them.

Several months ago, the daughter of the Red King pledged her support for Camelon and brought thirty thousand knights with her. The Round Table knights questioned her motives as she came without her father's knowledge. Her father only found out about it after Arcas had sent a messenger thanking the Red King for his daughter's help. The Red King sent his special advisor to train with the knights and serve as a liaison between the Red King and his daughter. Whatever plans the Red King entertained about seizing Camelon for his own benefit were foiled by his daughter's headstrong idealism. Many people of Camelon seemed impressed by her pageantry. She even managed to seduce Lance, who went to bed with her within the week. The love tryst lasted only a night before they went separate ways. Those who knew the couple said that both seemed wiser from the experience. It didn't take long for the other knights to discover the king's daughter recklessness. Meanwhile, Lance learned to avoid fanfare and choose women of less pretension.

Somehow the Red King's daughter managed to lose her composure and lost ten thousand knights to the Persian's relations, who handed the prisoners over to an occult group for experimentation. The Serpentine Federation directed the forces against Camelon, while an occult group from ancient Egypt did the dirty work. Informally as the Black Dogs from Sirius, these tormentors were derivatives from previous Serpentine experimentation. Though they appeared in human form, they were programmed for war and inhumane acts of violence. The Grays, who had mingled with the Viking royalty, were either left out in the cold or fell into the hands of the Black Dogs, who enjoyed practicing vivisection on the hybrids.

Ironically, the Persian youngster had given the weed to Pellinor to soothe his suffering after the death of his beautiful wife. He had not known of Pellinor's madness and the brutal treatment of his previous wives, who managed to escape him somehow. When the young Persian learned that his royal family had been practicing black magic since ancient Egypt, he ran away. The invitation to visit Camelon could not have come at a better time synchronistically. No one at Camelon realized that the extent of the danger surrounding the Persian youth. Pellinor's royal relatives wanted to silence the Persian nephew before he divulged their dark political associations. Somehow they infiltrated Camelon and attacked the castle from within. Luckily, Gamaliel had brought some mirrors to reflect their images and the intruders vanished at the sight.

The knights who rescued the Persian youth returned to the castle with disturbing news. They had found the dead, mutilated bodies of the Red Knights captured earlier. Only the Red King's special advisor survived and suffered almost as much as the Persian youth. They freed the advisor and brought him back to Camelon to heal.

Arcas recalled these sobering revelations as he paddled down the river. Today the Flower Children lulled the Roman encampment to slumber with the warm fragrance of gardenias in the air. He easily drifted towards the island undetected by the Roman soldiers. After banking his canoe, he walked to Morgana's stone cottage and met one of his relatives from the castle in Germany.

"Hi Arcas," his aunt greeted. "Ingrod had to get back to Germany quickly. She left Egressa at Camelon and brought her son to live here on the island. They figured that he would be safer here."

"I understand," he said ruefully. "The Bishop of Canterbury wants to arrange a marriage for me with Guinevere."

"How is Guinevere taking it?" his aunt asked.

"Well, like me, she already has her own arrangements. 'The bishop never asked us. Instead he fixated on this political breeding issue. By the way, didn't Constantine just have his wife and son executed? I don't think these people know the meaning of friendship."

"Yes, I know," his aunt answered. "The bishop will milk whatever influence he can from this crusade until he has western Europe under the governance of Constantine. He'll give the country over to the Turks, and that will be the last we see of gender balance for several millenniums. The Turks mistreat their women terribly."

"Yes, I know," Arcas echoed, lapsing into the simple, almost nonverbal communication that he shared with his mother's relatives. "Any news of Pellinor's quest?"

'Odd, you should ask," she replied. "He challenged King Lot to a duel and killed him. We lost another ally. His three sons by his first wife, the fairy, were devastated. They sought retaliation and Pellinor's army killed them all. The Round Table will miss these three knights."

"How did he ever get into a duel with King Lot?" Arcas questioned her.

"Well, I think that Morgane Le Fey, his second wife put him up to it. Pellinor insulted her and demanded that King Lot defend her honor."

"What! How did Pellinor insult her?"

"He said that she was no fairy. You know how Le Fey has been trying to eradicate the memory of King Lot's first wife and the rest of her people. She is very insecure."

"Oh, I see, Pellinor touched a sore point with her."

"Yes, and King Lot paid, though she may have been trying to get rid of him, too."

"She is on a little killing spree," Arcas surmised.

"Yes, but so is Pellinor, whether it is by accident or intention. It could be called criminal neglect," she answered.

Arcas loved listening to his aunt's wisdom. "I see," he said. "Where is Morgana?"

"Oh, she is off fishing," she replied.

"How is the boy doing?" Arcas asked.

"He's just fine," she told him. "He really likes it here with all the flowers. I think this is the happiest that he has been. He needs to play in the outdoors. The castles have been a little too stifling for him." Then changing the subject, she asked, "Have you met Ed? He's the Red knight who has been protecting us."

"Are you sure it is just protection?" Arcas laughed, having heard of this Red knight who adored his aunt.

"He's very handy and pleasant," his aunt smiled, clasping her hands together in subtle delight.

Arcas nodded. "Sounds like everything is going well here."

"Couldn't be better under the circumstances," his aunt said.

"Give my love to Morgana. I am returning home to Laticia and Joslin. Thank you for your help," he told his aunt before kissing her good-bye.

Then he hurried home to the little hut in the village.

Chapter Eleven

Luckily, some villains
Come and go

Tune Reference: *Viva La Vida*
----Coldplay

AFTER SLAYING LOT and his sons, Pellinor fled to the Mideast and chaos reigned in his abandoned kingdom. Meanwhile, Morgane Le Fey went on a rampage, destroying everything related to the Earth's spirit. Gamaliel boarded the remaining fairies on the dragons and sent them to MidEarth, near location of the fallen city of Atlantis.

"I am going to miss those fairies with their gifts of light and art," Arcas told Laticia late that night after their departure. "I'm not sure I like these changes."

"They will always be with the plants as devas," Laticia soothed him. "You will always be able to find them if you look."

"You are right," Arcas told her as he settled beside her in their bed. "It is just that it won't be so obvious."

"Only to some," she assured him. "You'll always be able to find them when you need them. We must focus now. Morgana warned us of another upcoming Roman attack within the next few days. Some of the Roman ships got past the Sirens. They discovered earplugs. We'll need to return to the Camelon Castle soon and be ready."

"I know," he said wearily. "You are right, again. Thank heavens that I have you to help me stay on track. I might just follow the fairies to MidEarth instead," he told her, planting a soft kiss on her lips before drifting off to sleep.

"I love you," she whispered moments later. Then she fell asleep shortly after she heard his breaths deepened with a heavy slumber.

The next morning they traversed an underwater tunnel to the Camelon Castle. The tunnel went underneath a shallow river, which appeared much deeper on the surface. Only a few knew about the tunnel, which Arcas used mostly for emergencies or when he wished to travel undetected. He and those circling around him wanted to avoid the two trumpeters, who heralded the arrivals and departures with their horns. The inner circle of knights considered them gossips and a nuisance worth avoiding. Those who made the news never could be sure which side the trumpeters served. They were unreliable and easily bribed. Although he would have personally preferred to send them off to work for his enemies, the two trumpeters comprised another thorny issue that Arcas had inherited along with the planet's salvation.

Today Camelon held a luncheon for the remaining knights of the Round Table. They came from many continents and provinces. The trumpeters heralded the arrivals to the delight of the spectators. The Red knights were from Viking Land. The Green knights came from the Celtic Lands. Black knights came from Italy. Although approximately seven hundred thousand of knights connected to the Camelon network, only several thousand were invited to the luncheon.

Arcas told them about how Pellinor's relations infiltrated the Camelon Castle to seize his Persian nephew and how the Viking king's daughter attacked them with her armies. Of the captured knights, only the Viking king's special advisor survived, barely alive when they found him.

Arcas told the knights of the Round Table about the horrific prison treatment offered by their enemies. He also mentioned how poorly they treated their relatives. The Persian youth died from unmentionable horrors inflicted during his imprisonment. "We are back in time to the games of dungeons and dragons. Though we ultimately won the intergalactic wars of the pyramid civilizations, thanks to the Fairy kingdom, the Trojans want to strike everyone in hip like they did the Hebrew Jacob. Joseph got us a foot in the door in Egypt. The underground from the Rome catacombs is preserved through the library system established at Rhakotis. We know from history that the Phoenicians don't know everything with their pyramidal money schemes derived from Lilith's invasion of Gondwanaland."

Then Arcas alerted the Round Table to the potential Roman attack by sea, and cut the luncheon cut short so that everyone could prepare. The attendees were not disappointed as Roman arrows showered the castle walls within two days. Legions from Antonine Wall provided land support for the Roman ships.

For several days Laticia worked beside Arcas on the western rampart of the castle. Then the Roman soldiers broke through and overran the castle. Arcas confronted the legions as Laticia ran for higher ground to release some weaponry on the Romans below. Meanwhile Arcas swirled Calibur in the air around him. Sparks from the sword threw the Romans off their feet and killed some of them. Another Roman soldier threw a boulder, which hit Arcas in the head, and he fell to his knees. He dropped Calibur, and a second Roman soldier kicked it out of his reach. Though sparks from the Calibur killed the soldier when he touched the sword, Arcas could not grab Calibur before falling unconscious from the head injury. He heard Laticia scream, and then his world went blank.

For a brief dull moment, Arcas dreamed of Flowery Meadows, and of finding Laticia reaching for him in the tall grass. Then he awoke and spied Gamaliel with Laticia on the higher level of the castle. Together they hurled popping firecrackers at the Romans, who had never been to China or Tibet. The loud sound frightened the legions and they quickly fled the castle. Arcas rolled over on his back and watched the mayhem in slow motion. Too weak to fight, he focused his energies on removing himself from the exodus, so that fleeing Romans would not trample him.

"Good job," he called to his wife and Gamaliel after the Romans had left. Laticia laughed and left her post to join Arcas, who had propped himself up over some sacks of potatoes. She kissed him before quickly assessing his injuries and stopped his bleeding with a piece of her torn tunic.

He returned her kiss, still feeling dazed from the shock of his injuries. She kissed him again, and he responded more fervently. He regained his strength in his legs and somehow found his way through the corridors of the stone castle to their quarters. They stumbled together down the halls, almost dancing and falling over each other. Alone in their room in the far turret, he slipped her clothes off and passionately caressed her warm body as she pulled him towards her. Within moments he went blank again, and time seeming stood still in their loving embrace.

He awoke in the early morning light with Laticia softly sleeping by his side. He gazed at the angel beside him and contrasted the chaos of the previous day, finding the difference between night and day. He closed his eyes as he gently wrapped his arm around her. Then he fell asleep again and dreamed of the Flowery Meadows.

Later that week, news of the Bishop of Canterbury's edict condemning all Briton pagans reached the Camelon Castle. Arcas read the edict at the next Round Table luncheon.

"Are we considered pagan?" one of the knights asked at the Round Table.

"Only those who have not been ritually sacrificed in the Mithraic mysteries are considered pagan. So apparently, by the Constantinople governance, we may be pagan, especially if we are tried in their courts. The mind-control programs of the invaders have returned. If we obliged their baptisms, then we became sainted for the concentration camps. Unlike like the others on the planet, we are descendants of those angels that arrived on platforms, instead of the refuge colony from Mars that landed on Sin. There's a reason why the desert of the Arabs resembles Mars, a planet once rich in vegetation and water. The Romans renamed the earth fragment called Sin. They call Sin, the moon. Our tradition comes from the archangel Michael through the lineage of Melchizedek, the king of Salem. Lilith perversely tied the earth's fragment to the feminine element in the Atlantean war to alter the genetic composition of the descendants of Eve. The Trojans at Nicea want to undermine the birth process and substitute their own ploys. Pain occurs when the ways of the body are not respected. All fighters experience pain; it tells us when we have done something wrong."

"What are courts?" another knight questioned. "It sounds like an Arabian witch-hunt for those who are not Hag's descendants. Ishmael called her Hagar. They want to restore the pyramid-economic structure by collecting the oil of murdered whales and take to to our posts in Connecticut. Many of Gilgamesh's descendants crossed the Bering Strait when ice rings circled the earth during the intergalactic wars. They still spend their time gambling for their future. A few strays reached the Anasazi and regained hope; they became known as the Hopi."

"Something that we haven't needed yet in our simple land of mutual respect and cooperation," Arcas replied, before changing the subject. "What is the latest word on Morgan Le Fey?"

"She pursues the Green knights now. Ley Fey doesn't like people who talk to the leprechauns. All the Green knights consult with leprechauns. She figured out that the leprechauns are cousins to the fairies."

"Will it be the rainbows next?" Arcas questioned with a sigh. "This woman needs to get a life instead of taking other people's. Maybe we should introduce her to the Bishop of Canterbury. No. Better not. There would not be a planet left if those two joined forces."

Then he rose from his chair, addressing the entire assembly, "I have something very important to say about the strategy concerning life and death transitions." When the room quieted, Arcas elaborated further, "No more transcendence, folks. From this moment on, we must give them a fight, even if it costs our lives. That's the game plan."

Commotion broke through the ranks, "Ah, do we have to...?"

"Yes, it is mandatory. We have to avoid those alien-white-light engagements and reduce the risk to our souls. Lance, here, proved that we could develop immunity through transcendence. We must pledge ourselves to the planet if we are to secure it. Enough said."

Without any more deliberation, he waved to the diners, "Excuse me, I gotta mend a few castle walls and prepare for the next Armageddon." Then he smiled and hurriedly left the dining hall.

Slipping out of the castle at dusk wearing a hooded cloak, Arcas went straight for the bank of the river. Not even the trumpeters had seen through his disguise. He searched the waters for the Lady of the Lake or one of her friends. Withdrawing Calibur from his cloak, he raised it in the moonlight. It glistened and cast a reflection over the water. Within moments, he spied the silhouette of the mermaid mother who had furnished the sword. She treaded in the soft light of the sword's reflection on the dark waves.

"I saw your signal," she told Arcas, as he put Calibur back in his cloak.

"I need to consult with you," Arcas said. "Terrible things are coming our way. I need your advice and help.

"Forget it. You saved the planet. I heard about the Round Table discussion. It is a very ingenious idea to fight to the death."

"Well, OK, but I need your help to pull it off. I ask for your protection during the transitions. We will most likely engage the Serpentines in direct combat; if any of us get captured. I shudder as I think of the torture. I remember the tales of the Arctos, the Bear sect that hid in caves. The parents of the captured children later found that the Serpentine Federation not only had conducted inhuman experimentation on their youngsters, but they had been raped, sodomized, mutilated, and impregnated. The dead bodies found in the labs told the whole gruesome story. These people do this sort of thing. They are not human."

"I agree. We can help with the crossover just as we did with the intergalactic wars of Egypt, where the dead were floated across the river like they do in India. The water weaves a special metaphor for the consciousness. We will make sure that no extraterrestrial race intervenes if you become part of the natural order. The spirits of the planet will harbor you across the consciousness into the next life."

"Also, if anyone is in an unwinnable position against our enemies, will you use natural forces for mercy so that they may avoid capture? I would hate to feed the Serpentine's experimentation. Life is not an experiment."

"Look at me," the mermaid demanded. "I am half water spirit and human. I wear the mark of Serpentine experimentation. You have my promise with all my heart and soul. Thank you for this opportunity to make right what was so wrongly done in the past."

"Thank you, blessed lady," Arcas murmured with a solemn nod. Then he turned and headed back to the castle as the mermaid slowly sank into the river."

Chapter Twelve

When the day arrives for action
Or the direction becomes clear
The forks in the road disappear
No more time to remain still
Right or wrong
Only those who fail to act
Lose their spirit

Tune Reference: *Don't Look Back*

----Boston

WITHIN THE MONTH, Elaine, one of the female Green knights returned from Maury's estate with a message. Being a swift runner, Elaine specialized in communication operations. She often ran cross-country from present day Marlboro, England to Rough Castle near Antonine Wall, Scotland. As a familiar sight on the terrain, locals began calling the barricade vacated by the Romans, Elaine's Wall, and she could often be seen running along it. Arcas spent most of his time near the Camelon Castle, known in present-day as Rough Castle. Racing inside the castle walls, Elaine found Arcas in the hall, where he entertained visitors.

Elaine told him that Maury supported the Bishop of Canterbury, because she enjoyed the religious discipline. Arcas received this news with mild surprise, already familiar with Maury's headstrong pursuits. However, he mentioned his disappointment that she could be so blind and easily influenced. He attributed the fault to the discipline that fed her warrior spirit.

"Obviously, Maury has lost her head. Tell Maury that she can have the Marlboro Castle as back up, only if she becomes more reasonable," he informed Elaine. At the time, Camelon consisted of a network of castles laced across present day Scotland, England, Ireland, and Wales. The Camelon Castle in Scotland outsized the Marlboro Castle by four times.

Ed the Red Knight who accompanied Arcas's aunt, entered the hall next. He addressed Arcas, "Your father went to the royal castle in Germany to aid your mother against an attack by Constantinople's forces. Your mother fought to the death, but your father transcended when four Serpentines cornered him."

Tears welled in Arcas eyes and he thanked Ed the Red Knight for the information. "How are you and my aunt holding up? And my godson? How is he doing?"

"We are doing our best. Your aunt has left the Flowery Meadows with your godson. I plan to meet her at one of the royal castles in the South Isle. The fairies and leprechauns have gone underground there so that Le Fey doesn't enslave them with her mind-control programs."

"That sounds like a wonderful idea," Arcas agreed. The South Isle existed in present-day Wales. After embracing the Red Knight, he stated, "Thank you, Ed for taking care of my aunt and godson so well."

Ed the Red Knight went on his way and Arcas left to talk to the intelligence officers in the south turret.

"My parents have passed on," he told Egressa and her apprentice. "Constantinople's forces brought in Serpentines to attack the castle in Germany. I hear that the emperor is ill and others are running the shop. The world tensions mount here. Northwestern Europe is being used as a distraction from the power grab in Turkey."

"I sense that Ingrod protected Ryan during his transcendence," Egressa said to Arcas.

"People are going out in two's," Igraine observed, uplifting the mood. "It's the buddy system."

Arcas sighed with relief when the responsibility lifted from his shoulders. Suddenly he felt at peace with this renewed perspective. "Thanks," he told them and walked away to gaze outside one of the turret windows. He could see the water in the distance and the forest opposite it. Then Arcas changed the subject. "Can you see why Pellinor invited us to meet with him over the breeding of his horses? It seems so trivial in these times and breeding is not practiced in this region. We prefer the wild ones. Something gives me an odd feeling about this social invitation. Pellinor is so touchy that I do not feel comfortable declining his offer." Stepping away from the view, Arcas took a deep breath and elaborated further, "He might make war on me like he did King Lot. My grandfather Cole met his death after meeting with Pellinor. The depth of Pellinor's support extends to the emperor himself. Then there is his murky association with the Serpentine Federation. Where does Pellinor stand on the issues? How did he do on his latest quest?"

Egressa stared with Arcas at the world outside another window in the room. "We can't see what is going on in that region for some reason," Egressa answered. "It puzzles Igraine also."

"Any word from travelers?" Arcas inquired.

"Nothing," Egressa replied.

"Shall we send an envoy to collect information?" Arcas questioned.

"No, I don't think that we would find out anything new," Igraine speculated. "It may be something that Pellinor only cognates on subconscious level without realizing it consciously."

"How about if we relocate to the Marlboro Castle. Give Maury a little extra support and provide back up for the visit with Pellinor. Maybe we could persuade him to exert his influence in changing the bishop's edict. We'll have help from the Morgana and some Druids there. I am not sure that staying at the Camelon Castle is our best position."

"It looks like the best move from our information," Igraine announced and Egressa nodded her agreement.

"OK, give me a day or two as I gather more information on this strategy before going forward," he told them.

Later that evening, he met Laticia in the hut for a brief dinner. Though four months pregnant, her figure still hid the pregnancy. Under the grave circumstances, she and Arcas kept her condition a secret between the two of them.

"I feel that I should stay here with the infants, pregnant women, and other health risks. The Red King's advisor is still recovering from his prison torture. They emasculated him and removed a third of his digestive system. In addition, they placed three implants in his body so that they could track his movements. I am having difficulty removing them in his weakened condition. If he accompanies you, then they could use him to detect your presence. They expect him to be with a doctor, so it wouldn't be anything out of the ordinary for Serpentines to notice."

Arcas thought it over for a few moments and consented. "From a family man's perspective, it would also hide your pregnancy. Only those who stay would notice the weight gain. You would be out of sight and out of the public's mind. Gamaliel and the local Druids can help keep on eye on things here."

The inhabitants of Camelon ferried across the waters to Castle Marlboro. Many had fond memories of the Yuletide feasts given in the area, and looked forward to being in the area for the winter. Meanwhile Arcas took a couple hundred knights and visited Pellinor's Castle almost a hundred miles away.

They had not foreseen the Time Line, weaved by three sisters, who had been enslaved by the Gauds. Some ancient civilizations called them the Fates. The oldest sister, Atropos, choose endings for people. The middle sister, Lachesis, determined the length of the life, while the youngest sister, Clotho, spun the thread for the life. Halfway on their journey to Pellinor, they crossed this Time Line, which had been manipulated by Pellinor's ancestors for generations. Pellinor served as the keeper of the Time Line. He set a trap for Arcas and the knights. His infatuation with the game of chess had compelled him to invite Armageddon on his property, so he could watch the endgame from his castle view.

Initially, the Time Line bewildered the knights. They lost their sense of direction at the crossing. It brought them to a time zone intertwined with the galactic wars of ancient Egypt. The Serpentines picked up where they had left off years ago and brought in their starships, ambushing the knights in the desert with technology that had been abandoned thousands of years ago. Pyramids loomed around them in the distance. Except this time war had not been declared by either side. Their weaponry stunned the knights and they were unable to respond. All the knights were captured and led out of the Time Line. Then scenery abruptly returned to the grass and trees native to the area.

The Thunder People responded with streaks of white lightning across the sky. The Bishop of Canterbury and his men eyed the lightning streaks in the distance and trembled slightly. One of the lightning bolts struck a dead tree and it burst into flames. A sudden gust of wind blew the flames across the forest where earth spirits fanned the sparks into a burgeoning forest fire.

Many of the Serpentines with a dominant reptilian brain panicked and fled. They deserted their prey, leaving the captive knights on their own. A gust of wind swept half of the stunned knights into the conflagration and they perished. The Serpentines quickly reduced the intensity of the stunning weaponry and ushered the remaining captives to the extensive prison underneath the Bishop of Canterbury's office.

The local church operated the prison, which served those who called themselves the "Illumined Ones." They specialized in a form of torture called mind control and spiritual annihilation. The Illumined Ones wasted no time in beating, chaining, and sodomizing the surviving knights, as they remained numb from the effects of the stun guns. By the time the effect of the stun guns had worn off, the knights were restrained in heavy metal chains.

The Bishop of Canterbury raped the king and then forced him to recite the Nicene Creed, beating him up whenever he missed a line. Then Pellinor came later and raped the king before challenging him to a game of chess.

"I'd give you a stronger game, if you would get me out of these chains," Arcas told him. Then he taunted, "All this time I had thought that you only wanted to be friends."

Pellinor ignored him and studied the chessboard for his next move. As much his foes wanted to steal the insights of his soul and mind, Arcas began to see deeply inside the machinations of their own soulless behavior. He realized that within the depths of his own soul that he had hit his limit with the torture. Having only lasted a few days before the daily rituals started to dull him, he decided to have some fun and mess with the oppressors' mind.

"Oh excuse me, I think I am going to puke..." Arcas announced, making sure to deposit the contents of his stomach over the chessboard. "Sorry about the mess. I think I just got you out of a checkmate though. No harm done."

Pellinor glanced at Arcas as he started to slowly wipe the vomit off his chess pieces. Still lost contemplating his next move, he eventually realized that the board had become too messy to view. "We'll play a new game tomorrow."

"OK, but promise to be gentle," Arcas chided him.

The next time that the bishop started beating him to recite the Nicene Creed, Arcas allowed himself to loose consciousness. The bishop became frustrated over the delay and lost his composure just before Arcas temporarily regained his senses.

"Sorry for the delay. I forgot my place. I feel so sleepy and my head hurts so much for some reason," he apologized before lapsing into another altered state with a slightly ecstatic smile on his face. Somewhere in another dimension, Arcas entertained sexual fantasies concerning the mother of his children. He dreamed about getting Laticia pregnant.

The bishop became jealous that Arcas seemed to be having more fun than him and started screaming, which brought Arcas out of his trance. "Did you say something, Bishop?"

The bishop fumed and left the room. He hadn't slept in months.

Within the week, they unchained Arcas and threw him in a cell with the rest of the surviving knights. He landed beside Tristan and Lance on the ground.

"What happened?" Tristan asked. "We heard the bishop's screams and became worried that they had killed you."

"I had too much fun," Arcas answered with a wide grin, before a chuckle rolled from his insides. Seeming satisfied with himself, an expression of self-contentment came naturally to him. In the end he could not help but be himself.

Tristan laughed deeply and Arcas heartily joined him until they were almost delirious. The rest of the surviving knights couldn't help but smile, despite their pain.

Chapter Thirteen

Hidden from the fairy tale and the myth
Is a stark reality and truth
That separates the children from the adults
And distinguishes the loves of our lives

Tune Reference: *In My Arms*

----Plumb

MAURY LEARNED OF the capture through the village near Marlboro and she sent an assistant to inquire at the bishop's office. When the messenger arrived at the bishop's office, he heard screams from a small window from the prison underneath the nearby church. He peered inside the opening and almost fainted at the view inside. He quickly left the scene and hurried back to tell Maury about the horrific treatment that the knights received under the bishop's authority.

Maury's partner became aghast at the news and packed the youngest children for the Castle Camelon. Meanwhile, Maury contacted the intelligence operations at the Marlboro Castle for news about the capture. Although Arcas had offered her the use of the Marlboro Castle, she remained sitting on the fence of her estate. Having been unsure what Arcas meant by the gesture, she shuddered her understanding of the message. Arcas had conveyed his suspicions of Pellinor, offering whatever means available to provide help in the instance that something happened to him and Tristan.

Well, she thought, *something had happened*. Though not in immediate danger, Maury would be their next target after they destroyed their prisoners. A religion had been concocted to justify the genocide. She helped her partner and children pack and sent them off for refuge at the Camelon Castle.

Being slow to act under the present political circumstance, Maury arranged an audience with the bishop. Although she remained on amiable terms with him and not fully committed to Camelon, Maury confronted the bishop on the captured knights, which he tried to deny. When he became angry, she quickly changed the subject to the bishop's travel plans for spring vacation. When he informed her that he had no vacation plans, she blinked with the realization that the prisoners were in for a long haul. Meanwhile, she tried to gather as much information that she could about the local clergy and elusive guards around the premises. She looked for a weak link in the defenses. When Maury let the bishop know that she had relocated to Marlboro Castle, the bishop raised his brow. Without elaboration on the subject, she implied that she benefitted from Arcas's absence.

Relaxing, when he made the wrong assumption, he confided, "The emperor's advisors in Constantinople want all prisoners crucified at the end of the summer. I have been busy with preparations lately. They don't want any survivors."

Maury almost choked on her mead, but recovered and asked, "What prisoners would merit this treatment?"

"Oh there are a few who would create political embarrassments," he speculated before excusing himself from their meeting. "I'll see you at the service this Sunday," he told her as he led her out of his office.

As the days passed she learned more information about the fate of the rest of the knights. The majority of the army had been ambushed on the way to rescue the prisoners. The huge river that separated the Marlboro Castle from the town of Canterbury had a thick layer of ice, solid enough to hold five times more people than the thirty-thousand knights that crossed it that day. When huge laser guns appeared out of the sky to evaporate the knights, the ice beneath their feet suddenly broke. All the knights in the vast army were towed underneath the frozen water. The lasers misfired, killing some of the dark warriors.

Being bright, Maury trusted that the forces of nature had saved their souls from annihilation at the hands of the Serpentine lasers. Thrown back on her own spiritual resources, it took her two months to decide whether to free the imprisoned knights. Then she took another month to devise a foolproof plan with only a handful of people to help. She determined to rescue the knights only after she could no longer ignore the village whispers about the terrible things that were happening beneath the church. The whispers had grown into a roar by this time. A few villagers had confronted the bishop on the matter. They disappeared in the night and were never seen again. An eerie silence hung over the church and an exodus had started among the townspeople. Meanwhile, the bishop put guards around the street level entrance to the prison. He no longer hid his role in the tortures from the townspeople. Becoming more brazen about the nature of his activities, even his own guards became victims of his brutality.

Seizing control of the moment, Arcas used his unchained time to boost morale and comfort the prisoners, who grew closer to each other as a result of their experiences. His training with Laticia had taught him how to use his hands in setting bones, stop bleeding, and easing pain in traumatized sites. He taught these techniques to the Black knights, who shared the cell with him. They shared these skills with the others in different cells.

"Don't worry about those Black knights' kisses," Arcas whispered to Tristan one afternoon after Geraldo showered Tristan with affection when he returned from the daily torture. "He's Italian. They are very exuberant in expressing their emotion. Besides, it makes the pain go away. I'd kiss you, too, but they chained me to the wall again. Word got out at how good I am with my hands, and now I can't touch anyone. The bishop gets jealous."

Tristan shook his head and laughed a little. The light humor distracted him away from his painful predicament. He took a deep breath and relaxed a bit.

Villanti couldn't help but overhear their conversation. The next day when the prison guard attempted to chain Arcas to the wall after the morning torture, he seductively slipped his hands around the guard's throat.

"I love this man, and if you chain him to the wall one more time then I will kill you."

The guard heard the soft voice connected to the strong male arms. He relented in bewilderment and terror. Dropping his grip on Arcas, the guard turned to face his attacker, who towered over him. Then he fled.

"You're the man," Arcas, shot back, rubbing his aching but free wrists.

Tristan roared with laughter, and Eilene smiled wryly. Bridget stayed on the ground with a broken hip from the last rape, and moaned a light response. Geraldo held her in his arms and massaged her lightly.

Then Villanti eyes dropped to the pool of blood around Arcas's feet, drawing Arcas's focus to his own body. Arcas shrugged and sponged up the blood with the end of his tunic.

"Beautiful legs," Villanti commented.

Moved by the nonviolent interaction between the two men, Eilene suddenly kissed Tristan softly on the cheek and hugged him with one arm.

Tristan pulled her lightly towards his own body in response, then released her. Arcas lowered himself on the ground and feel asleep beside the rest.

After a month of continual torture, all the prisoners died spiritually and went to another dimension, leaving behind only a shell of the human being that they had once been in life. Some fell into despair; others became the lightest of spirits. Pellinor began to complain and cry that everyone had left him. Though their physical bodies remained, even Pellinor could detect the absence.

Meanwhile, they began placing implants in the bodies of the prisoners. These were special implants designed to stay with a spirit through future lifetimes. Canines hated the implants and would attack the soldiers who had them. Those who had special relationships with the animal kingdom, such as the Green knights, were the first to get them. The technicians from the Black Dog group tested their results by allowing dogs in the prison to maul those with the new implants. Then they chased away the dogs before the victim died.

"You cans see why we never invited these people to our Druid fires," Arcas remarked to Tristan several weeks after his physical body had turned more ghost-like. The entire cell overheard his rally, and the rest of the cells echoed with Tristan's hearty, rolling laughter. By this time the oppressors counted six people in their cell. Two female Green knights from Celtic Land, named Elaine and Bridget, shared the cell with the Yellow Knight from France, Tristan, and two Black knights called Villanti and Geraldo. Arcas knew to keep conversation light, and Tristan's laughter proved contagious. If he could get Tristan to laugh, then he knew that he would start, too. This really irritated the prison authorities, who tried to promote intimidation and terror.

"I am *so* not into this," Arcas rejoined another day after the daily ritual torture. "Now every time I look at Pellinor, I puke. Can't help it. Comes naturally now, though I think that he is beginning to take it personally."

Tristan chuckled lightly, and Eilene grinned. Even some of the guards smiled at Arcas's dry humor. Arcas had worn them down, too.

"They say that we won't be seeing each other anymore," Arcas winked and smiled at Tristan, who broke out into roaring laughter. Even Galahad, the Blue Knight in the next cell, cracked a slight smile. Lance's eyes glistened at his words and celebrated one less tortuous experience. Though imprisoned, Lance possessed a powerful immunity and the guards didn't touch him. Dry wit and not taking oneself seriously thwarted any attempts that the torturers made at mind control. Even the bishop gave up trying to get Arcas to learn the Nicene creed.

"They just have a very different lifestyle," the bishop tried to explain to the messenger from Constantinople. "I am not sure I understand it all, but I think that I can get more details with more time."

Meanwhile the bishop spent less and less time with Arcas, who seemed to be on another planet whenever he approached him. He envied the joyous camaraderie among the knights. The bishop needed the distance to avoid being swept into the mirror that Arcas held for him. He had seen the depths of his own bitter emptiness, and it began to eat at him, though too far down his path to be sidetracked. He remained loyal to the Serpentines, as if somewhere in his soulless universe he could find some life. Being a victim of the Grand Illusion didn't bother him as long as he had a place, even if it meant an endless quest or thirst for things that amounted to nothing.

The rest of the knights caught on to Arcas's tactics and adopted them for their own use. Meanwhile Arcas continually gazed at the small porthole to the outside world and visualized it getting bigger and bigger. He imagined it getting so big that he would be able to escape through it. This is how he entertained himself when he wasn't busy talking Tristan out of mild hysterics, keeping Eilene from getting bored, or humoring the prison staff in the hopes of humanizing them. His mind focused on his escape, and the first step towards that goal involved surviving the present experience.

Though unaware of the extreme state of the prisoners, Egressa pressured Maury to rescue the knights. Sensing their ghost-like condition, she told the queen that they would be tortured to death. Despite Egressa's pleas, Maury continued to deliberate and procrastinate because she knew that she did not want to seal her fate with the knights. Even if she succeeded in freeing the knights, no army remained to fend off further attacks. The authorities at Constantinople would pursue the knights until the end just like they did with Pellinor's Persian cousin. They did not want anyone alive who might divulge their dark networks.

Eventually Maury decided to pursue her connection with the Michael matrix, the network of Light Beings who provided safety from the Serpentine Federation and Black Dog Occult Group. She met an altar boy named Michael after one of the services, who seemed oblivious to events beneath the church. Carefully choosing her words, she approached him. "Michael, do you know the people who live underneath the church?"

"What people?" he asked.

"The ones who need my help," she told him.

"Oh, they are ill," he acknowledged with a sigh, playing dumb. The young altar boy had Druid parents, and he joined the clergy as a way of exerting his influence from within. A bright student, he possessed an adept understanding of both worlds, the Druidic and the Christian.

"When will the infirm see the light of day?"

"They are scheduled for the cross three weeks from this day."

"Blessed they may be. We will call on Saint Michael to deliver them from their afflictions when they see the light."

"On that blessed day Saint Michael will set fire to the south end of town where he blesses the bishop's livestock with his presence."

Maury grinned slightly when she heard his words. She stepped back a little to regain her composure. This young man cared for the bishop's livestock, and the bishop valued his horses more than anything else in life.

"Give this holy medal to the tallest Yellow knight who goes by the name of Saint Tristan. He is the sickest one yet and needs holy protection from Saint Michael," she said, pressing a medal of Saint Michael in his palm.

The young man clutched the medal in his palm and looked up as if in prayer. Then he blest her and asked, "And who shall I say sends this prayer?"

"Mary, a holy virgin of compassion," she told him, purposely modifying her name. She genuflected slightly and hurried away in the crowd.

Three weeks later, the knights saw daylight for the first time in over four months. The bishop and a Salish prince from France marched the prisoners from their cells and into the public square. The townspeople gasped when they saw their condition. They were the walking dead without a flicker of soul's light in their eyes. Instead their feeble bodies radiated a soul light so powerful that it hung over the group like a single halo. Those who were unable to walk were carried by some of the other knights. They appeared more as angels than as warriors.

They marched the knights to the town square. Underneath the town square could be found an underground library of ancient secret knowledge. Pellinor had stumbled upon the library during his excursions in the bishop's prison. Though Pellinor attempted to study the materials collected there, the knowledge somehow failed him. The stacks of manuscripts on the shelves were never intended for someone like him.

Once the knights had passed over the site of the underground library, their plight changed. The guards placed a wooden stake in the hands of Arcas. Suddenly, Arcas became electrified and swung the cross around as a weapon. Unaware of its use as a spiritual symbol in ritual murder, Arcas had heard of the cross from tales of the Spartacus rebellion, which did not have any spiritual merit. He knocked over several of his captors, and the prisoners began their escape in the commotion.

Within minutes the town heard the cry from a clergyman standing near Tristan. "Fire in the holy stables. God save the holy horses!"

People looked in the direction of the stables and saw a flames dancing in the southern sky. More commotion ensued while the clergy and guards ran for the stables. The prisoners untied themselves and ran off in many different directions.

"You get your horses, and I will seize what belongs to me," the Salish prince told the bishop. Then he jumped on his horse and rode into the throng towards Tristan.

"You defector!" he yelled at Tristan as he tried to follow his path in the chaos.

The prisoners escaped during the mayhem. Michael handed Tristan the medal and lifted Arcas onto to Maury's stallion. He had fainted from exerting himself physically in the struggle for freedom.

"I'm in charge now," Maury stated. "Tristan, head for the castle where reinforcements will meet you. Arcas and I will provide a decoy."

Arcas moaned as he slowly regained consciousness. When he found himself in Maury's arms, he brightened considerably. "Oh Maury, it's about time you make up your mind," he moaned.

Maury smiled slightly at her friend's recognition, but she knew that she had an angel in her arms. Arcas didn't have much life left in him and might not survive the ride away from town. For a brief moment, she recalled how often they had ridden together in childhood. All that practice together had paid off at this precise moment.

"I have Calibur," she whispered to him. "You can find it in the saddlebag when it is time to fight."

Michael had retrieved Arcas's sword from the pile of weapons in the bishop's storeroom. When the weapon glistened in the moonlight, Michael figured that the sword belonged to Arcas. He smuggled it out and gave it to Maury the week before the prison break.

Maury rode for the plains west of Marlboro. She hoped to cross the sea to the Camelon Castle before the bishop caught up with them. The Romans would not follow them across the waters where the merpeople would destroy them.

Chapter Fourteen

BRIDGET THE GREEN KNIGHT

The strongest never cry
They find relief in the
Loves of their lives

Tune Reference: *Don't Cry*

----Seal

ALEC THE GREEN Knight carried Bridget out of the town square. He recognized Maury in the crowd and watched the interaction between Michael and Tristan. Sensing that Maury ran with Arcas to distract the Romans, he followed Tristan closely behind. When he noticed the Salish prince trailing Tristan, he decided to find another route to the castle.

Bridget had suffered a broken hip while in prison and had passed out from the pain during the march to the town square. Alec carried her as far as he could, but he became too weak to continue the journey with her on his back. Fortunately, a riderless horse happened to appear in front of him. Frightened during the mayhem in town, the stallion instinctively headed for Marlboro Castle. Alec placed Bridget over the horse and secured her on it. Then he slapped the horse's buttocks and directed it towards the castle. He was too injured to ride, and she was too injured to walk. For the moment, putting Bridget on the horse seemed the best solution possible.

Bridget slowly regained consciousness later in the evening and found herself on top of the horse. The horse had paused at the edge of the forest before risking exposure on the treeless hilltop near the castle. Bridget took the horse's reins and stabilized herself on the horse. Sitting sidesaddle due to her hip, she sat upright and studied her surroundings. She had a vague memory of having been freed from prison and figured that her friend Alec had placed her on this horse for safety. She sought refuge under the cover of a huge oak tree, which seemed to shield her from the scene on the plain before her. Gazing at the horizon, she spotted Tristan and several other knights clashing with guards from the town.

Her father had been a Druid King of the O'Connor line, who had assimilated some of the Trinitarianism Christian practices in Ireland. This Druid King had helped the Patrick the Red Knight lead an insurrection against the Serpentine Federation. Patrick had once been enslaved by Morgaine Le Fey in her attempts to eliminate those strongly connected to the earth spirits. When the Vikings began to incorporate the Grays in their lineage, Patrick fled and connected with the leprechauns and fairies. Morgaine Le Fey captured him along with them.

The Druid King became allies with the Trinitarians after they were shunned from the Council of Nicea. Constantine's advisors wanted to separate the religion from the spirit of the earth and developed the creed for this purpose. The Trinitarians aligned themselves with the earth spirits, which included the leprechauns and fairies. The Druid King aligned himself with the Trinitarians, and they became allies against Morgaine Le Fey.

In her youth, Bridget had been the Keeper of the Fire in the Druidic tribe. All the encampments used flames from this fire to keep their own hearths warm. She found that she preferred passing the torches with the wood of the oak tree because it seemed to withstand long distances without burning out. Though not every Flame Keeper favored this tree, Bridget cultivated a special synchronicity with the oak. Like the oak torch, the Celtic people felt that Bridget nourished an eternal spiritual flame. She had infiltrated the slave camp and given a shamrock to Patrick to wear so that his allies could identify him. They freed Patrick the Red Knight and helped him throw off his captors.

Morgaine's son and favorite henchman, Mordred, had been skulking in the shadows along with King Pellinor in the town square. When the prisoners escaped, Pellinor ran away in fear of retaliation from those he had tortured. Morgaine Le Fey had instructed Pellinor in the manner of how the knights were to be crucified that day. For his part, Pellinor demanded that the Bishop of Canterbury crucify his prisoners. Morgaine Le Fey had altered the ritual murder to sever the knights from the spirit of the planet.

After Pellinor fled and the knights escaped, Mordred tracked the Green knights to carry out his mother's business. His mother had made a deal with the Serpentine Federation to destroy the Green knights. He followed the Green knights through the various tracking devices that had been implanted in them during their imprisonment. To fulfill his mother's wishes, Mordred developed the rabid instincts of a mad dog and used these senses in a predatory manner.

Within a day, Mordred spied Bridget the Green Knight fighting on a plain. He signaled his men to join the opposition. Bridget had left the cover of the oak tree and charged into the battle alongside Tristan. Swinging her sword with the power of a mighty oak, she took out some of Mordred's forces as well as some of the Salish. Facing death in the eye, she continued to fight despite her hip injury.

For eight days, they battled on. Then the leader of the Salish resorted to sorcery. He stunned the knights with a powerful weapon that he had borrowed from Pellinor. Pellinor had manipulated the Time Line to retrieve one of the technologically advanced weapons. The Salish leader threatened to kill Pellinor if he did not give it to him. Although Pellinor abandoned the weapon, he cursed on the Salish leader so that his life would end if he used the weapon.

The weapon stymied Bridget, and Mordred's forces seized her. They knocked her off her horse and drug her across the plain to the top of the hill. Her captors drove huge metal stakes into the rock to pin her down. They arranged her limbs in variation of the pattern often used by native basket weavers, a symbol used since the Great Ice Age, eleven thousand years ago. In the Chinese *Book of Silks,* the symbol described the comet of the Great Cataclysm after the fall of Atlantis. Serving as a symbol of eternal life, the Chinese employed it later to describe the eternal balance of Yin and Yang. Bridget's assailants reversed the ancient symbol of life, transforming it into a right-armed swastika representing planetary destruction, the ultimate Serpentine goal.

When Bridget recognized the meaning of the reversed symbol she contacted the earth spirits. The earth spirits contacted Queen Mab, leader of the water spirits and sister of the Lady of the Lake. Queen Mab peered into Bridget's dreams like the flow of a river. She entered the knight's consciousness while she lapsed into altered states due to the intense pain of the ritualized murder. She sensed the knight's heartfelt request for balance and harmony rather than destruction. Queen Mab balanced the fire within the stoic knight with a river of tears.

Rain began to violently fall on the hillside. Bridget's captors ran from the heavy rain droplets, which bathed her and eased her pain. The river below the hill began to swell and rise above its bank. The rain continued to wash the terrain. Several neighboring rivers flowed past their banks and added more water to the river below the hill. Then the current gathered in speed until the force of the water freed Bridget's limbs and swept her body downstream. The fast-moving waters engulfed her, and she drowned quickly. The next day, the river deposited her body in a hawthorn bush growing alongside the sandy bank.

The celestials on the island were aghast at the evidence of torture written on the body of the knight. They contacted Gamaliel, and he flew a Furry dragon to Camelon Castle to find Laticia. Together they flew the Furry dragon to the Flowery Meadows south of Marlboro. There, they learned of the crucifixion and collected Bridget's body for the funeral pyre. Her death served as a warning for the inhabitants, who underestimated the degree of violence erupting in the region. They eyed the wasted Roman soldiers on the Avalon fort with renewed suspicion. A third of the celestials stepped forward to join the fight, knowing that those who favored security over freedom soon lost both. They entered the Camelon forces as the Pink knights, truly representing another dimension.

Bridget's father, King Duffa of Leincaster made the journey from Ireland to pay his final respects. He brought reinforcements from the Druids, earth spirits, and Trinitarians. More Green knights entered the foray. Within two days, one of the newly enlisted Green knights spotted Mordred's body washed on the banks of the Roman settlement at Avalon.

Chapter Fifteen

TRISTAN THE YELLOW KNIGHT

Those champions

Who never learn to lose gracefully

Never seem to win

Despite all the dues paid and

Mistakes admitted

Tune Reference: *We Are The Champions*

----Queen

TRISTAN LEARNED THAT his enemies from France had caught up with him when the altar boy handed him the Saint Michael medal from Mary. His grandmother, a Frank and a member of the royal family in present-day France, had married a Salian prince aligned himself with the Roman Empire. As their grandson, Tristan had spied his relatives practicing black magic with the Roman spiritual leaders. Disliking the Roman occupation and the the effect on Gaul, and he left the clan. His relatives pursued Tristan as a defector because he could bear witness against dark secrets. When he served as king of present-day France, they sought to control him.

The Saint Michael medal held special significance for Tristan, who knew that the effect on the magi would be the same as a crucifix on a vampire. The reflection of Saint Michael dissipated their negativity, which usually was all they had to offer. As a result, the entity would disappear. The Saint Michael medal proved a powerful tool, and not many people knew about this application.

Tristan ran out of the town square and found a stray horse. Mounting the horse, he rode away towards the Marlboro Castle. He raced the horse across the plain to the castle, where he was cornered by the Salish prince's soldiers. They engaged him in battle, and he flashed the medal in the sun. The reflection from the sun lighted their faces. His assailants shrieked. Within a minute they disappeared and he galloped away.

Further across the plains, he encountered more magi. They told him to dismount and yield his sword, which he taken from the disappearing magi behind him. Unfortunately the Saint Michael's medal did not work as well this time because these magi were only obeying orders of the initial group. However, the sword that he had taken possessed greater magical power than the swords of the underlings. Brandishing his sword in the sunlight against his opponents, he killed them all quickly. Then he galloped away across the plains.

Next he spotted a group of Roman soldiers who were only carrying out the orders of the preceding magi. He looked in the sky above him and noticed Igraine's white owl flying overheard. He knew it was a message to turn around before the Roman soldiers saw him. He followed the owl into a thicket, where he foraged for some wild edibles near the stream. Then he waited for the soldiers to pass. The owl nested in a tree overhead as the soldiers passed from view.

After the soldiers had left the area, the white owl led Tristan out of the thicket and along the edge of the plain. Soon he saw the Marlboro Castle in the distance, and the white owl departed for the southwest turret. Walking to within one hundred yards of the castle, he stopped. An arrow whizzed right by him and landed on the ground a few feet away. He recognized the bowmen as guards from the town square. Tristan sped his horse towards the drawbridge and inside the castle walls. Jumping off his horse he went straight to the southwest turret to search for Igraine.

"Thank you so much for the owl's protection," he said. "I didn't think that I would live to see this castle again."

"You arrived just in time to help defend it," she commented. "The Romans will probably make an attack on it tomorrow." Igraine noticed that the knight becoming emotionally upset and changed the subject to a lighter topic. "Egressa is out running errands within the castle. We are expecting the arrival of few more knights. King Gawain is three days away and he has a thousand by a thousand fold, which is at least a million bowmen and spearmen. Time is on our side."

Despite her reassuring words, Tristan became hysterical. "What about Robert, my uncle from France? He is a warlock now. They have been following me since the escape from the town square. I can't believe he is getting away with it. Somebody has got to stop him."

"I can't get any information on him," Igraine answered, trying to calm down Tristan. Though Arcas could calm Tristan better than she, Igraine gave it her best effort. Seeking to help the knight protect himself against an archrival from several past lifetimes, she advised, "You need to disguise yourself both inside and outside of the castle. Your uncle is very angry with you for leaving him. He fears that you will betray his secrets."

"Somebody's got to get him," Tristan repeated. "I know that he is doing terrible things."

Tristan's persistence caused Igraine to wonder how this feud had ever started. She watched the Yellow knight exit the southwest turret as quickly as he had entered. He rushed to figure out a disguise that he could use inside and outside the castle. Finding his way to his former quarters in the castle, he entered the familiar room and rummaged through some of his old things for an idea. For some reason, he sense that the Saint Michael's medal would not be enough to stump this warlock.

As he pondered the choice of his disguise, he suddenly heard a shriek outside of his window. He quickly dropped his things and looked out his window for the source of the cry. From his window he could outside of the castle walls to a lightly forested hill below. He saw a woman being accosted by a henchman of unknown nationality. Grabbing his sword, he raced out of the castle to confront the henchman. To his surprise, he discovered that the unidentified woman was his sister and the henchman was his Uncle Robert.

"There you are!" his uncle yelled, raising his sword at Tristan. The woman laughed at the deception, which had successfully lured Tristan to the warlock. Then she also brandished her sword at Tristan. Tristan quickly ducked and ran away from the raised swords, while his Uncle Robert unwittingly brought his sword down on his niece instead of his nephew. The woman screamed again before she fell to the ground in a pool of her own blood.

Tristan ran back towards the castle as the uncle knelt over his slain sister. His horse came running out and met him most of the way. The trumpeters had sent his horse to him, after he paid them handsomely to protect him. Tristan quickly mounted the animal and again safely made it into the castle.

Igraine met him in the courtyard as he walked the horse around to cool down.

"I've missed several attempts on my life today," he observed. "So far I've been lucky."

Igraine nodded and peered into the distance. She wondered how long his luck would hold in his present emotional state. His rival proved a very cunning dark wizard.

"How about just taking some time to rest," she suggested. "It may help clear your head."

Tristan agreed and went back to rest in his quarters. Glancing outside of his window, he saw that his uncle and sister had both disappeared. He reclined on his mattress and dozed for an hour. Then he rose and wandered outside of the castle while still in a semiconscious state. He dreamed that he had heard his destiny calling outside of the castle walls and had gone outside to determine if it was the destiny he really wanted.

Darkness began to mark the end of a long day. The trumpeters had been paid off by Tristan's enemies to hide something in Tristan's drink that would cause him to wander in his sleep. Something about the darkness helped Tristan fully awake from his deep slumber. Then he remembered that he had forgotten to don his disguise. Within moments he found himself surrounded by his enemies on horseback. Fortunately, he soon found himself aided by other knights. The battle began and he lapsed into another altered state as he clashed swords with his opponents. He could fight in his sleep, having learned the maneuvers so well that they came automatically without thought. Fighting well and endlessly, Tristan extended the evening battle and it lasted a little over a week.

Then one of those laser guns from the Time Line stymied him. The Salish seized him and pinned his body to the rocky hillside. Metal stakes held his body in the shape of a traditional cross. Rain began to fall in torrents and rivers ran their banks. His enemies fled for higher ground and his Uncle Robert left with them. The raging waters engulfed Tristan and he quickly drowned before the current ripped his body from the hillside.

Gamaliel retrieved Tristan's body from another hawthorn bush on the bank of the Flowery Meadows, a day after recovering Bridget's body. The waters receded when the storm ended, and Gamaliel waited for more bodies to wash up on the shore. The silent corpses told similar stories of their torment. The remains of their enemies also rested on the shores of Avalon. The Salish had suffered silent heart attacks after employing the weapon stolen from Pellinor's Time Line.

Chapter Sixteen

ALEC THE GREEN KNIGHT

Carrying a bitter wound
The only release is in the
Motion of time

Tune Reference: *Only Time*

----Enya

ALEC HAD BEEN imprisoned along with Patrick when Morgaine Le Fey seized the leprechauns and fairies on present-day Ireland. After Patrick escaped, he returned for Alec and freed him along with the rest. Alec's Druid parents had been tortured and killed by the religious clergy in the area. When they took his parents away to the local church for torture, the four-year old boy had gallantly tried to rescue them. He blocked the door to the hut and raised his little sword as the soldiers exited with his parents. A Roman soldier slashed the young boy's face, leaving a permanent scar that forever haunted his handsome features. Orphaned, Alec became a slave. The enslaved fairies and leprechauns adopted Alec and raised him as one of their own. When he matured, his adopted family dubbed him the "Green Man."

After his release from the slave camp, Alec joined Patrick in studying for the priesthood. He became knowledgeable in the Christian discipline as well as the Druidic and Celtic. Not only possessing a stronger spiritual fiber than Patrick himself, Alec had a heart of gold. Being a perpetual scholar, he eventually decided to train as a Green knight with Bridget. When Patrick became bishop of the region, Alec journeyed to Camelon with Bridget and Elaine, and became the third Green Knight of the party.

Though he knew how to connect with every bird, bee, and flower, his anger raged deep inside. Failing to understood those who intended to destroy the spirit of the planet, he used his anger to shield himself from his torturers and endure. Targeted almost as much as Arcas, his enemies remembered his role in freeing the fairies. Alec could disguise himself as a green bush and spook the Roman horses. The Romans started seeing his face everywhere in the understory, and the image haunted them. When the bishop's soldiers captured him, they were irritated to discover that it was only the Green Man from the Celtic slave camp.

After sending Bridget off towards the Marlboro Castle, Alec ducked in the understory to rest. Having been conscious during the implant procedure in prison, he suspected the devices served as tracking devices. Unlike Arcas, he understood the significance of the cross given by executioners. They intended to crucify the pagan in the manner of Joseph's son. Arcas never had the time to learn any other spiritual discipline besides common sense. The king behaved as a true innocent in the town square. The religious clergy became stymied by their own feelings concerning the religious symbol. Arcas probably had wondered why they had given it to him. What others saw as a cross, Arcas saw as a weapon.

In prison, Alec had suffered extensive abdominal and spinal injuries, which made travel by horseback uncomfortable. He would have to make his way to the castle by foot. Thinking his plan though, he reasoned that walking by the river towards the castle would afford him more protection because of the dense underbrush. Slowly he made his way to the river, which flowed out of town and downstream to the castle. When he reached the bank, he uncovered a canoe from a thicket and paddled to the castle. Armed with the knowledge that most Roman soldiers didn't know how to swim and avoided the water wherever possible, Alec stayed near the river. Some of his acquaintances partnered with the Roman warriors and told Alec stories about them. Most of the Roman soldiers were gay and sought partners outside of the Roman army to avoid political complications. Unlike the Celtics, the Romans suffered from a deficit of strong women in their culture. Centuries of abuse had destroyed their female role models and left them without a swimming instructor.

Almost two-thirds of the way, Alec saw Mordred's army crossing a bridge ahead of him. He stopped and hid in the tall verdant grasses along the river. They marched across the bridge and hurried towards a hilltop in the distance. Lost in their focus, Alec's presence escaped them. After they had disappeared down the road, Alec continued paddling downstream and watched Mordred's army head for the hilltop instead of the Marlboro Castle. In their driven fury, they never tracked his implant.

At the foot of the Marlboro Castle, he stepped out of the canoe and hid it in some reeds along the bank. Rushing out of the Time Line, Pellinor's relatives suddenly appeared and ambushed him. They had waited for his canoe to make the last half mile.

"We meet again," a dark wizard announced.

Alec didn't respond, nor did he bother fighting the soldiers who seized him. They quickly tied his arms to together and led him to the hilltop. Then he understood what was going on. He watched the skies grow dark and the rain begin to fall. The river that he had navigated began to rise and cover the hillside. The bridge that Mordred's army had crossed quickly washed out.

All this happened before he reached the hillside with Pellinor's dark wizards. Meanwhile, he saw the nature spirits at the edge of the forest. Their shiny lights dotted the vegetation and comforted him. Understanding that they would help in the end and he relaxed, appreciating the friends he had in other places.

He saw Bridget already pinned to the hillside and bowed his head. Alec understood the meaning of the symbolic representation of her pinned body and noted the reversal. The rain fall harder and harder while the nature spirits danced in the nearby forest. The forest dance, as old as Shiva the Hindu goddess, reminded him of his travels to India with Patrick. There, he learned of Shiva's dance of life and death. Imitating the rhythmic moves of Shiva, the dancer learned how to move through destruction. He had observed this dance at Shiva's temple along with the other Trinitarians. Now it inspired him in his present challenge.

Further up the hill, he saw Mordred's army try to nail Tristin to the rocky outcrop. Alec's captors pushed him past the scene. Though the rising river had already covered Bridget's body, his assailants didn't seem to mind. Their obsession drove them to their fate as much as they led Alec to his destiny. The knife that cut the thread of the Time Line for this event transformed into a double-edged sword. He wondered if the dark wizards had realized this. Unlike him, they did not have friends in other places.

Near the top of the hill, Alec observed the torrent rip Bridget's body off the hillside and drown Tristan. The dark wizards remained blind to the whirlpool developing around them. Knocking Alec to the ground, they haphazardly staked his arm and foot before one of them screamed.

An explosive wave from the rising tide encircled the legs of the dark wizard just as he raised his mallet over one of the stakes. He screamed as the white wave knocked him off balance and pulled him into the undertow. The other dark wizards came to their senses with the scream. They stopped their activity and tried to rescue their accomplice, who soon succumbed to the violent waves. Then they panicked and tried to learn how to swim the hard way. Nobody in their culture had ever taught them.

After all the dark wizards on the hillside drowned in the raging waters, the rain came softly and waters rose calmly. Unable to free himself, Alec relaxed and easily drowned within minutes. A day later, the river raged again and pulled his body from the hillside where it floated to the banks of the Flowery Meadows. Laticia retrieved Alec's body from a hawthorn bush near the place where Gamaliel had collected Tristan's body earlier that day.

Chapter Seventeen

DABIN THE PINK KNIGHT

In the most despairing moments of life
Search for the grace of just hanging in there

Tune Reference: *Everybody Hurts*
----REM

WHEN EGRESSA SAW Tristan wandering out of the castle in a semiconscious state, she alerted Igraine and the rest of the Intelligence group in the southwest turret. Then she summoned her falcon and directed the bird to the Flowery Meadows. The falcon followed the light reflected off the red stone on her ring and flew to the Flowery Meadows. The people in the castle could see the flooding on the far away hillside but could not make out the activity there. The vague uncertainty left them with a horrific sense of grief and loss.

Morgana showed the falcon to Dabin, one of the leaders of the Pink knights. His appearance differed from anyone else's on the planet. Dabin's shoulder length pure white hair possessed a translucent quality such that the hair shone pink in the daylight. Celestial airships could easily spot him from above, and he kept his hair shoulder length for this reason. Dabin waited for the falcon from Egressa, who would give the signal for his Dragon flyers to fly out to the shataquah around present day Avebury. The Pink knights hid a few Furry dragons on the Flowery Meadows for emergencies and this was one of them. Igraine met them at the shataquah. She had left the Castle at Marlboro through a portal, another emergency procedure.

When they received the orders to move the manuscripts from the old shataquah to the ancient library underneath the town, Dabin sent some of the Pink knights to the underground library with the books. Meanwhile, he and Igraine moved some of the structure to present-day Stonehenge. They used the Furry dragons to help move the structure while the others rode to the underground library on the horses that Igraine had secured.

The shataquah consisted of a thatched dome with a hole in the top for a variety of purposes such as smoke, light, or energy outgassing. Stone structures supported the thatched dome and were place in circular arrangements. Not only did they use the shataquah for Round Table meetings, it served as a school for alchemy studies. In addition, it provided the energetic power source for the Camelon network of castles, as well as the collection of sacred caves in present-day Tibet. The ley lines connected with the most sacred mountains of the world. The base provided the energetic glue for the entire planet, which had been in place for the intergalactic wars of ancient Egypt. At the time, many of the stones structures were composed of superradiant, ormus materials, which could not only levitate, but they could reappear and disappear. Once he had delivered the structures to the new site, Dabin placed the most important one in a state of disappearance so that only those individuals with the correct energy or chi could find them. In other words, only those who practiced internal cultivation could empower the stone grid. After finishing with the new site, Dabin sent the riderless Furry dragons to the original base on the Druid Isle. Then he joined the group that transferred the books to the underground library.

"We have complications," they said as they greeted him. "We found Pellinor hiding among the library stacks. We don't know how many other uninvited guests have access to the library."

They brought Pellnor to the leader of the Pink Knights. Pellinor took one look at the pink-haired knight and fainted.

"Just as well," Dabin softly replied.

The Pink knights allowed Pellinor to collapse to the floor unaided. He hit his head on the metal shelves, and those around him felt assured that he would not be regaining consciousness anytime soon.

"Take him to the nunnery on the east side of town. I know the Mother Superior there from the earlier days when Romans destroyed her Druid village. Tell her to extract any knowledge that she can from this intruder as part of the information exchange. When he regains consciousness let Pellinor know the terms of his refuge. If he fails to cooperate, kill him. This Mother Superior will be able to handle him. I know her well. Then meet me at the Marlboro Castle."

Two of the Pink knights flanking Pellinor hauled him out of the underground library and to the nunnery. Dabin made another trip to the shataquah with the remaining Pink knights. He transferred as many books as possible to the library before the shataquah fell in the hands of their enemies. A shataquah proved more difficult to hide than the underground library. He determined that Pellinor had not told his associates about the library beneath town square.

"Look, Dabin, there's Egressa's falcon," one of the Pink knights shouted as he pointed high in the blue sky above them.

With only a few more books remaining to be transported to the underground library, Dabin noticed gathering storm clouds in the southern part of the sky and stopped. On his last trip to the underground library, he energetically sealed the entrance, causing the library to disappear. The entire library, including the building, shelves, and books were composed of ormus materials and could be placed in other dimensions. Dabin left the shataquah with the other Pink knights and then looked for Igraine.

"Almost everything has been moved. We will have to let nature take her course," he told her.

Igraine nodded quietly. The castle expected a direct attack soon and everyone prepared for the inevitable conflict. "Many of the escaped knights are still trickling in to help defend the castle," she told him. "Can your forces help them make it back? We will need everyone possible. Keep yourself safe, too."

Dabin smiled and hugged her good-bye. He went on his way through the corridor. Summoning his Pink knights, he told them about their next mission. The Pink knights nodded their understanding as they listened.

However, Egressa quickly interrupted their strategy session. "I've just received word from the Lady of the Lake that the bishop's soldiers have captured Morgana and she is at the gallows at the town square. They torched the Flowery Meadows."

Dabin and his Pink knights gasped. They hurried out of the castle and rode into town as fast as they could. A huge fire had swallowed the gallows. The fire that had been started in the Flowery Meadows had gone out of control. High winds had blown the flames across the river and into town. The entire southwest portion of the city burned.

"What happened?" Dabin inquired of young altar boy, who was hauling buckets of water to fan down the flames in the town square. Ash and perspiration marked his brow.

"Morgana perished in the fire before the bishop could behead her as a witch," Michael the altar boy told Dabin as he wiped his brow. "The flames rose so high that even the bishop's stand caught fire. He fled with his men, but the woman sitting beside him burned to death. They called her Guinevere and she planned to marry Arcas. When he died, she would be crowned queen of the United Kingdom with the bishop's blessing."

Dabin's eyes misted when he heard the news of Morgana's death. He took a deep long breath and continued, "Thank you, my friend for the news. Can you tell me your name? I think I knew your parents long ago on the isle."

"My name is Michael. Yes, you probably did know my parents on the Druid Isle."

"Good luck to you, Michael," Dabin said before he rode away with his Pink knights.

Dabin reflected on the sudden events in the town square that had just occurred. They had been as quick as the fire that fueled the changes. Both the bishop and Guinevere were celestials that gone dark, whereas Morgana served as a celestial warrior of the light. Both of the women had died in the recent fire. Guinevere's sister, Maury, possessed the strength of forty men inside her slight frame. Whether Maury had chosen the dark side remained to be seen.

"That's a significant investment in this agenda to be the queen of England," Dabin remarked to the Pink knights around him as they rode out of town. "They have completely ignored the conditions of the sword in the stone, which is probably why the Lady of the Lake embedded Calibur there in the first place. She knew that this struggle for leadership would occur, even amongst the celestials. With leadership comes responsibility. These other contenders forget this part of it."

His companion agreed. Turning onto the road heading towards the Marlboro Castle, one of the Pink knights interrupted their thoughts. "Look there is a White knight. He's been wounded, and he almost falling off his horse. It's Sir Kay, one of our knights trying to make it to the Marlboro Castle."

When the group got closer to the White knight, they saw that not only had he been wounded, but he was crying. The Pink knight, who had spotted Kay, raced to offer assistance. "Oh my," the Pink knight said gently. "You're arm is bleeding." The Pink knight began to administer first aid as the White knight collapsed into the arms of another Pink knight. They pulled the rest of his body off the horse and had him lie down on the grass.

"Can you tell us what happened?" Dabin asked as the groggy White knight regained his senses.

"I ran from the town square and right into an army of Roman soldiers. I stole a sword and a horse and then killed them all. Then I hid in a barn to get out of the rain."

"So why are you crying?" the Pink knight inquired as he tended to the injured arm.

"I don't know," the White knight replied. Wiping away his tears, he continued, "Maury the Silver knight took Arcas away with her. I am afraid that she'll take him to the bishop."

"We'll still here," Dabin responded. "Arcas can take care of himself with Maury. They have a long history, you know."

Kay took a deep breath and the tears ceased. "I know. You can never guess what to expect from those two. I was their instructor for several years."

"You've had a long day," the Pink knight observed. He finished bandaging Kay's arm. "Here, ride with me and we will tie your horse behind us. We need to get you to the Marlboro Castle. What is a White knight without a castle to defend?"

Kay brightened and smiled a little. They helped him on the Pink knight's horse and rode to the Castle Marlboro. At the castle, they were warmly greeted by Igraine.

"So happy to see you all," she said, hugging and kissing everyone. "I heard about Morgana...even Guinevere..." Then she noticed Kay's tear streaked face and quickly changed the subject. "Oh, Kay, what's wrong?"

"They spiritually maimed Arcas in prison. I don't know if he'll ever come back, even in another dimension," he began sobbing, hating to loose one of his best students to oblivion. Arcas was also his younger cousin, and he mourned him almost like a brother.

"We'll figure out how to help him avoid oblivion," Dabin comforted. "I have friends in high places. Come rest. We have a castle to defend."

Igraine patted him on the shoulder as she led Kay to his quarters. "Now don't go wandering in the night. Stay here and rest. Let us help each other. We can talk about Arcas after you have had some sleep."

As Kay rested, Dabin left the castle to look for more wandering knights. They camped in the forest for the evening and brainstormed on places where they might find more knights. Early the next morning, Kay came galloping into their camp.

"I've come to join you," he announced. "The castle doesn't need defending yet. I think I know where some of them might be. Some were recaptured by the Roman soldiers and are on the road to Avalon. They are being guarded by Pellinor's dark wizard friends, so we must be careful."

"That's enough to make me cry," the Pink knight said. Having found Kay, he hated the thought of dealing with dark wizards.

Kay nodded.

"Here goes," Dabin proposed. "Let's go find that road to Avalon and some of our knights."

Soon they had found the road to Avalon and the Roman soldiers. In the middle of the formation were three captured knights: two Black knights and a Green knight. The party of Pink and White knights wasted no time in attacking the marching soldiers. They clashed swords and broke up the formation as Kay and one of the Pink knights freed the others. Then they placed swords in the hands of the freed knights, who quickly made themselves useful.

Unfortunately, Pellinor's relations had booby-trapped the Roman soldiers with a remnant of the Time Line. As the knights fought the soldiers, time went faster and faster until a powerful vortex encircled them. Within the vortex, lightning bolts streaked across the air. Some of the people within the vortex were ignited briefly into flight. They sailed in the air across the atmosphere and landed softly on their feet. The atmosphere remained calm in the eye of the vortex, but a wall of turbulence prevented those inside from exiting. People moved faster and faster inside the vortex. Then Kay watched Dabin vanish into thin air, which literally seemed very thin at this point.

"Dabin!" Kay screamed. "Dabin, come back!"

Dabin reappeared briefly when Kay called for him. When time sped up again, he disappeared.

Realizing that he could call him back and make him reappear, Kay yelled again. "Dabin, come back!"

Dabin reappeared, but only for a moment. One of the Roman soldiers knocked Kay to the ground. Elaine the Green Knight slew the Roman soldier and Kay got back on his feet. He called for Dabin again, but could not reach him.

The knights killed all the Roman solders trapped with them in the vortex. Time slowed down as the battle ended. The knights continued calling and searching for Dabin as the vortex dissipated. When the vortex had completely vanished, they found Dabin's body on a field twenty-five yards away. Although, they found no wounds on Dabin, he was obviously dead.

They carried the body away and placed it on top of one of the horses. Then they rode back to the Castle Marlboro. Igraine congratulated them but cried when she saw Dabin's body. They placed it in a room where she could examine it more thoroughly for signs of trauma, which oddly seemed to be missing.

"I don't know what happened," she told them after her examination. "I sense that we might find clues at the old shataquah site."

Then she turned to Kay, "You were the last to see him go and you were the one that could call him back. I think that you would be the best one for the visit to the old shataquah. You tracked his energy better than anyone else. Go to tomorrow after you have had a good night's sleep."

Early the next day, Kay journeyed to the old shataquah site. In the remaining stone structure, he found Maury and Arcas. They had been camping there for the past two days.

"Dabin disappeared into thin air," Kay told them.

"I know," Arcas responded. "I viewed him during one of my open-eye meditations. He entered the deck of an airship."

"We found his body in a nearby field. We took it to Igraine at the castle. She can't figure it out."

"I can," Arcas said.

Surprised by his answer, Maury stared at Arcas.

"We went to the same dimension," he told them. "I am still alive on this plane, but not quite all here. He is all there, but he will come back in a different form. I am holding the space for him in both places. We have reached our limits. I spiritually died in prison, and I am not afraid to admit it. Maury is the exception here. She has obviously has chosen to keep her celestial ways. Dabin and I are truly only human and must stick to the rules of nature."

Maury appeared rather sheepish with Arcas's words. She sighed with the admittance that she never got much past him. He always patiently waited for her to reap the consequences of her decisions.

"We need to hold a torch for Dabin, so he can find his way. Give it a day or two, and wait for a sign. It will probably be something in pink. Tell Igraine this. Have her light a candle at the Marlboro Castle."

With his instructions, Kay quickly turned and mounted his horse. Then he faced Arcas with his departing words: "We will light a candle for you, too."

Chapter Eighteen

KAY THE WHITE KNIGHT

There is a profound difference between
Emotional goals and spiritual ones

Tune Reference: *Come Back To Me*
----David Cook

"DON'T FORGET TO light one for yourself," Arcas murmured as Kay disappeared into the early morning sun. Keeping his voice low, he declined to inform his former instructor that he wasn't all there either. Kay had spiritually died with all the other knights in prison.

Kay had been his first role model as a knight. His cousin was the son of his father's brother, who also had been a Red knight and a Dragon flyer. Kay's mother had been a Druid on the isle and served as a Dragon flyer. When Kay was only two-years old, she died on a mission near Marlboro. His grief-stricken father gave the boy to Gamaliel to raise along with the Merwyns. As a young boy, Kay raised the Furry dragon nestlings just as Arcas did later. He had also operated the old shataquah site near Avebury, which also served as a base for the Dragon flyers. Though safe enough for a small child to operate, they dismantled the base under duress.

The regional knights were the Silver knights. Those who served without compensation were known as White knights and they served the ideal. Kay's parents had made him a financially independent warrior. Being a nonprofit knight, he held a special purity within the knighthood. For this reason, they called him the White Knight.

Kay hurried back to the Marlboro Castle to tell Igraine the news.

"Got it," she replied. "I can light the candles here, but I have something for you to take to the new site. I think I have a pink candle that I can use for Dabin…"

Igraine knew that she was on the same wavelength as Arcas now. She understood the silent reason why he had sent Kay back to her with the message. The new site on present-day Stonehenge needed a new foundation, and this White knight could help establish it with a pure hand. Kay followed Igraine to her southwest turret where she quickly told Egressa about Kay's mission. Immediately she and Igraine flurried about the cylindrical room gathering bottles of different flower and sea essences. Waiting for Igraine, Kay sensed what they were doing but didn't bother tracking the details. Instead, he relaxed and savored the new energetic lightness in the room.

"Here," they said as they handed him several flasks with instructions. "This blue flask is for the perimeter of the structure. It is a special mixture for protection. Spread it around the circumference."

Then Igraine handed him a violet bottle. "This one is for the center. Dump it there so that all those who enter the circle can find their own center reflected within."

Egressa handed him the final bottle. "This green one is for the spirit of the Furry dragons, who must disappear soon from the earth plane. We go with them in many ways. It represents the highest level of spiritual development found on this planet. Let the winds diffuse it around the site."

"Yes, I think this should cover it," Igraine remarked as she patted Kay on the back, pushing him on his way out the door.

Kay accepted the parcel of colored bottles. Lost deep in thought, he reflected on all his past memories associated with the shataquah. He only vaguely remembered his mother, who would hold him in arms on the fine, furry beasts. Kay had left the Avebury shataquah after his mother's failed mission.

He inspected the energy of the place and the connections made there, how it gridded all the Dragon flyers to the planet, so that they could find their way back in spirit, no matter what terrible things happened to them. That had been the nature of his childhood. Terrible things happened, but there was a limit, an underlying belief that everything turned out right in the end. He could still feel his mother around him whenever he visited the site. The shataquah served as a safety net, and the stone structures were arranged in such away to resonant with the harmonics of the universe. It served as the most coherent waveform in the galaxy, bonding the planet to the universe.

As his thoughts turned over in his mind, Kay found something amiss. They needed to account for the holographic universe. The holographic universe represented an alternate reality dependent on the mirror reflection of resonant frequencies. Not only did souls need to be centered, protected, and inspired by the highest forms, but they needed to be able to find themselves in the positive reflections of another. Maybe Dabin had forgotten this when he placed the invisible structures within the new Stonehenge site.

When he arrived at the Stonehenge site, he stepped into the rings of the stone formations, and the hidden structures materialized as easy as flipping a switch. The hidden structures consisted of tubular clay stones specially made from ferrous materials. People had fun making them and infusing them with the frequencies of different uplifting energies. He could remember those days. The activity resembled a class project, but it spanned the lifetime of the planet. Each generation added an infused tubular structure to the collection of stones.

These tubular casts were hollow inside and could amplify a particular frequency through the process of supperradiance. These energies were gridded into the ley lines of the earth. Some people referred to these energetic points of reference as dragon lines. The Furry dragons only flew into regions where the energy was coherent. This served as their protection. Otherwise they flew directly straight into MidEarth through some cave in present-day Tibet, where the monks could guide them in mediation.

Kay inspected the site and found that Dabin had missed placing the holographic connection, probably one of the reasons for his untimely disappearance. He pondered over how he could correct the situation. Where could he find himself in this structure?

He visited the most recently infused structures for the information contained within, but he could find nothing that reflected his present situation. Then he walked to the center of the circular formation and found that the water from the violet bottle had formed a small pool. Staring at his own reflection in the small pool, he saw his face reflected in the color belonging to kings. His blood relation, King Arcas, served as the Purple Knight. Within the hue of color, Kay saw a glimpse of the king within. Then a thought form permeated the purple haze and Kay recognized himself. The frequency in the crystalline fractal pattern of the water molecules spoke to him. It told the story of someone who had compassion. The face looking back at him showed the face of someone who cared. The face expressed freedom of choice with *compassion*.

Though almost paradoxically, Kay recalled the light that created the planet originally. The earth rose out of darkness, created by the Light Beings. Kay smiled at his reflection, nodding as he rose from his knees. Then he left the shataquah confident that it contained everything needed for the next realm. Rather than survive, life needed to thrive.

Kay mounted his horse and rode towards the Marlboro Castle. He found the castle under siege. An unruly association of dark forces had decided to attack at once, probably the only thing they would ever agree on. Without a moment's hesitation, Kay jumped into the fray. He fought gallantly and stood his position. Nobody could get by him, and he pushed the forces away until they called for a retreat to the river below. For a day or two, fighting ceased as the opposing forces regrouped. Kay entered the castle and met Igraine looking for him in the courtyard. She hugged and kissed him after he dismounted.

"You did it!" she exuberantly told him. "Hologram and all. We picked it up."

Kay smiled. He had found an inner peace, a growing confidence in himself that could not be taken by any foe. His face radiated this new spirit, and he infused those around him with this knowledge, shattering their despair.

The attacks resumed the following morning and Kay mounted an offense outside of the castle. Again, they pushed the dark forces back to the river. This time they pushed harder until their foes were on the other side. Kay pursued them across the river as the sun set in the west. A pink hue streaked across the sky, reminiscent Kay's friend Dabin. A well-placed arrow from the other side pierced his heart, and he fell into the water. He drowned before the arrow took his life. The river carried his body downstream and to a bigger confluence. Days later, Gamaliel found his body entangled in a hawthorn bush on the Druid Isle.

Igraine witnessed Kay's demise from the southwest turret, and her prayers went with him downriver. A white candle burned for the White knight on the small table near the window. His efforts succeeded in bringing peace to the Castle Marlboro for two more days. This gave Gawain's reinforcements more time to reach the castle.

Chapter Nineteen

MAURY THE SILVER KNIGHT

Cherished memories of fun and laughter

Pierce the dark days

That separated us

Tune Reference: *Old Days*

----Chicago

MAURY WATCHED ARCAS shake and shiver during the nights that they camped together. Too weak to make the trip to Camelon, she honored his request to rest at the old shataquah site.

"You should leave and move on," he told her after Kay left. "The bishop will come after me sooner or later. He will scour the countryside for me. I am more important to him than the Marlboro Castle."

Maury deliberated, unconvinced that the bishop wanted to kill Arcas. She waited with Arcas to the bishop on this issue. The bishop had been a family friend for many years. He promised to make Guinevere the queen of the United Kingdom and make peace with Constantinople. He might thank Maury for bringing Arcas to him.

Unlike the Pink knights, Maury did not know that Guinevere had died in the fire while waiting for Morgana to be beheaded. The bishop wanted to destroy the female spiritual leadership in the Camelon network before introducing Guinevere as queen. Being Guinevere's younger sister, Maury held the English throne. She also didn't know that King Gawain the Silver knight raced to Marlboro Castle with a million knights. King Gawain would not accept Maury as ruler over Scotland. Any ruler that the bishop sponsored could be easily persuaded to take over neighboring countries. The bishop took orders from Constantinople's armies.

One evening Arcas awoke from a feverish sleep and told her, "I dreamed that King Cole told me that Morgana had died and that he was taking her into the next life. Do you think it is true? Do you think that the Romans attacked the Flowery Meadows?" he asked in a minor delirious state.

"No, no, no," Maury said. "I'm sure Morgana is fine."

Arcas shook his head over his concern for Morgana. The dream had been too vivid to discount. He sensed that Maury envied his position as king over all of western Europe. She had been really miffed when he became ruler after pulling the sword from the stone. Their relationship had become more distant. She never understood how he had managed to become king. For his part, Arcas could never figure out why she had never managed to pull the sword from the stone herself. Maury's father had been king of England and respected Arcas's rule over his kingdom. After his death, the kingdom had been divided among his four children. Maury's youngest brother died shortly after his father, leaving the kingdom divided among the remaining three.

Finally Maury abandoned Arcas at the shataquah and went to consult her younger brother. She betted that Arcas would be there until the bishop found him, too weak to travel and too focused to die. She reasoned that the bishop would attack the castle rather than search for Arcas.

As Maury neared her brother's estate, a group of knights heading for the Castle Marlboro greeted her.

"I am sorry about the death of Guinevere," one knight said with sympathy.

Stunned by his words, Maury insisted, "You must be mistaken," she told him.

"Oh, you didn't know...Well, never mind us," another knight said politely. No one ever wanted to challenge Maury, especially if it might lead to battle. He knew that she had the strength of forty men packed in her small frame.

"Gotta hurry," another knight interrupted. "Best wishes to you."

Then she remembered Arcas's dream and an eerie shock came over her. Trembling, she continued her journey to see her relatives. When she arrived at her brother's estate, she found everyone in mourning.

"What happened?" she inquired of the estate manager. "Where is my brother?"

"Your brother is burying your sister Guinevere. Didn't you hear the news? She died in the town fire. She sat right next to the bishop during the day they tried to behead Morgana."

Maury bent her head forward and caught herself before she almost collapsed to the ground. Failing to understand what had happened, her head began to swirl with the shocking information. The estate manager observed Maury's reaction. He had known her since she was a little girl. He tried to comfort Maury while helping her understand the circumstances. "They say Guinevere went to the dark side," the old man told her. "She wanted the bishop's help in becoming queen of the United Kingdom."

"But she was going marry Arcas," Maury cried.

"No, no, Maury," the old man told her softly. As the only one beside Arcas who could reason with Maury, he persisted. Unfortunately, Arcas had become a hot topic for Maury ever since he released Calibur from the stone.

"You know Arcas has a wife. The old ways do not formalize partnerships like they do now where marriages are arranged for political purposes. A tryst at a Druid Fire does not constitute a partnership. It is like a first date. Arcas spent another Druid Fire with Egressa, but so have most men, including myself. He settled and lives with Laticia out of free choice, just like you do with your partner. Remember, you are not married either and you had your partner's three children."

Maury bowed her head. The old man had a point.

"Arcas might have settled with you, but you shut him out after he withdrew the sword from the stone," the old man pressed her. "You became blind to his qualities like you became blind to right and wrong. You always questioned him and nobody else, even when he was the one who produced the miracle and earned the right to be king. It took a special kind of force to extract the sword, whether he wanted all that came with it or not. You must respect the fact that other people want him and what he has to offer."

Maury sat down on a log and began rubbing her head. She had spent a couple of fires with Arcas before he settled. Where had she gone wrong? It was as if they had never been lovers. Now her family had fled and over half of her father's family were dead. Guinevere had left the Druidic Fires for the beds of politicians, including the bishop's. Everything good she could ever remember about her youth was dying. Even Arcas was dying.

She rose from the log and kissed the old man on the head. Drying her tears, Maury resolved to do whatever she could to save a world that had meant so much to her.

"Remember," began the old man as smiled with Maury's blessing. "All the world's a stage, and the men and women the players in it. So go play, my child. Do not be afraid of drama, unless it is overdone."

Maury brightened and almost laughed at his words. "Like all the other celestials, I know, you have always been ahead of your time. Take what you can from the estate, and hide in the sacred mounds. Stay in the foothills outside of town until this scene is over."

Queen Maury the Silver Knight mounted her horse and returned to the site of the old shataquah. She found Arcas standing again and walking around the stone structures that had been left by Dabin the Pink Knight.

"You are looking more like yourself now. What happened?" she asked him as she hugged him.

"Oh, I centered myself in the middle of the shataquah and a time traveler appeared. He wore a turban and carried a carpet under his arm. We went for rides on his magic rug and flew over the countryside like the old Dragon flyers. After we landed the magic carpet back at the old shataquah base, he bowed and told me: "*Namaste*. I honor the place in you in which the entire universe dwells; I honor the place in you that is of love, of integrity, of wisdom, and of peace. When you are in that place in you, and I am in that place in me, we are one."

"That's huge," Maury commented. A few magic words and a carpet ride had revived Arcas.

"Yah, I know. Then the time traveler took off on his magic carpet. I feel much better just knowing that someone else in the universe who understands what we were trying to accomplish here."

The approach of the bishop and his army outside of the shataquah interrupted their conversation. The clanking of swords and the heavy steps of marching Roman soldiers could be heard. Arcas drew his sword and met the bishop in the field. No longer determined to confront the bishop, Maury delayed inside. Through a small opening, she glanced at the untouched Castle Marlboro, which remained second on the bishop's to do list.

"We meet again," the bishop greeted as he motioned his men to raise their swords. There were approximately four hundred of them. Arcas shrugged at the bishop's army. Nothing scared him anymore.

"I want to know this man's crime," Maury demanded as she stepped onto the field beside Arcas.

"There is no crime, you fool. It is Armageddon. I have brought aliens and their gods to assist me."

Arcas moved closer to challenge the bishop's proposal. Technically advanced weapons appeared in the background. Small tanks surrounded a giant tank with a laser gun protruding from its armor. Maury gasped. The bishop suddenly lowered his sword to strike down Arcas, and Maury the Silver Knight swiftly moved to protect the king. Arcas turned to fight off the army that swirled around him with the bishop's signal. He heard Maury scream as her neck took the brunt of the bishop's blow. He slew the bishop and his four hundred soldiers with his sword Calibur. Then four minutes after Maury's scream, a black arrow appeared from the edge of nearby forest and pierced his left lung and spleen. He fell to the ground as the galactic weapons advanced and aimed for the Castle Marlboro. Arcas hurled his sword at the giant weapon and jammed its axle. The machine exploded and caused the adjacent weapons to catch fire. The advancement stopped as the metal melted and scorched the ground underneath it.

Arcas glanced at the black arrow and understood that several armies supported the bishop. The black arrow belonged to a soldier from the league of shadows. Arcas realized the folly of this league of shadows, which sought to save the world by poisoning it. They had naively used the bishop for their self-righteous purpose of clearing the world of pagans, but had missed seeing the biggest criminal of all in the process.

Arcas lingered on the field and waited for help to find him. Gamaliel and Laticia arrived with Maury's brother an hour later. They studied the scene around them as they stepped over the bishop's dead body to reach the knights. Maury's brother carried her body and decapitated head away from the field, while Gamaliel and Laticia examined Arcas.

"Won the war; lose the battle," Laticia whispered to him as she held his hand. She knew that Arcas could not longer see her in his semiconscious state, though he waited to hear her final words on the subject. Laticia watched him relax and sensed that he had heard her. Tears rolled down his face as he recognized her presence. He pressed her hand lightly. Gamaliel cradled Arcas's head in his hands and applied some light pressure to his cranium. Feeling secure in Gamaliel's hands like he had as a small boy, he quietly took his last breath.

Leaving his body behind, Arcas's spirit rose and he saw Maury waiting for him a few yards away. She stood in the glow of the setting sun. "Time to go, Arcas," she smiled brightly at him. Her healed body had brilliant luminance that warmed him when he saw it.

He turned in the direction of Maury's nod and watched Gamaliel sling his body over his shoulder like a sack of potatoes. Then they searched the field for Calibur. He saw Laticia retrieve the sword from the middle of the burned area. The advanced technology had gone where it came from--- thin air.

"Let's go," Kay and Dabin echoed as they waved at Arcas from the end of the field.

Maury and Arcas turned to face them and joined them in the setting sun.

Chapter Twenty

GERALDO THE BLACK KNIGHT

Sometimes keeping a relationship
Can be a matter of life and death

Tune Reference: *How To Save A Life*
----The Fray

BACK AT THE Castle Marlboro, the knights watched the fireball in the sky over the old shataquah site. They never saw the machines explode, only the burning remnants thrown overhead. Geraldo nodded and pointed to Villanti, the other Black knight, who served as his reality check.

The two Black knights had met on the road to Camelon before crossing a river near the border to Scotland. Villanti came from the vineyards in northern Italy. Geraldo came from a small town in the middle of Italy called Cerchio, named for the small theater (*circo*) in the heart of town. They became fast friends and shared a love of wine and pasta.

Like Villanti, Geraldo had defected from the Roman army at Avalon and joined the knights at Camelon. He joined the Camelon mission for political relief. Geraldo's hometown in Italy hailed him as a hero, and his family waited for news of his activities with Camelon. They communicated through the theater's portal in Cerchio.

After reaching the Castle Marlboro with the remaining Pink knights, Geraldo and his friend Villanti had embarked on a little investigation on their own. They never missed an opportunity for intrigue and their little investigation of the rooms within the castle walls proved fruitful. They found a secret room. Figuring that Igraine knew about the secret room, they decided to confront her. Together they raced to the southwest turret and knocked on her door.

"Hey Igraine, what is so secret about the room hidden behind the trap door in the dining hall?"

"Oh that," Igraine answered nonchalantly as she opened the door and ushered them in the room. "It's a secret," she added absentmindedly. Her attention focused on the tarot cards spread on a nearby desk.

"Oh, you do the tarot!" Villanti cried, leaning over the cards. "My mamma taught me when I was just a little boy."

"We are here to ask about the secret room," Geraldo gently reminded him in a serious voice.

"We can ask about the cards too," Villanti insisted.

Igraine dropped her train of thought to fathom the meaning of the drama taking place with the two men. Unaccustomed to their exuberant manner, she paused and deliberated which topic to address first. Deciding quickly to ignore them, she gazed outside one of the windows in the turret and considered the meaning of her tarot spread. Apparently there were two traitors in the castle. They had already been paid off, and the betrayal involved a pair of trumpets.

Villanti slipped beside her without disrupting her countenance.

"Ask Geraldo, he's psychic," he said quietly and nodded at the view out the window in a knowing way.

Igraine eyed him carefully and resumed staring out the window.

"I know. The two trumpeters have been bought by the league of shadows," Villanti continued. He assured her, "Trust me."

"What you really need, Igraine, is a good night's sleep," Geraldo advised. He pulled her away from the window and lightly directed her to a small bed in the corner of the room. "We will come back tomorrow to ask about the secret room. C'mon, Villanti, we need to continue our tour of the castle. Let's go."

Villanti agreed and left Igraine just before she collapsed on the bed. She fell asleep in only a few minutes and dreamed about the explosion in the sky, which somehow pertained to Arcas.

After putting Igraine to bed, Geraldo and Villanti returned to the secret room near the dining hall. They spent most of the evening exploring the rooms. The Black knights discovered many more secret rooms.

"Hey Geraldo, maybe these secret rooms are for hiding in case the castle is attacked."

Cocking his head side to side, Geraldo considered this explanation. "Isn't that a little too obvious?"

Later that evening, they left the secret rooms and went to sleep in separate quarters. Geraldo awoke the next morning and hurriedly dressed. He met Villanti in the courtyard and had a quick breakfast.

"Hey Villanti, I have a feeling about those secret rooms. I think they are like the portal in my hometown. Let's go back and see."

Then they hurried back to the secret rooms and discovered that they were holographic. A three-dimensional image of the exploding plume over the old shataquah formed in the atmosphere in front of them. The room amplified thought forms and projected them into a three-dimensional reality, where they could be played out in different scenarios. Though the holographic images were ghostlike and only shadows of the forms in realities, the display of thoughts around an individual produced a startling sense of surrealism. Sometimes it could be difficult to separate dreams from reality. The viewer needed to be very solidly grounded and clear about their goals. Rather than spend much time playing in the holographic rooms, they decided to get Eilene the Green Knight, who being Celtic, possessed a solid stance in both the dream world and real world.

"Eilene, my love, since you believe in leprechauns and rainbows, could you help us figure out the images forming in the secret rooms?" Villanti asked.

Geraldo gently took her arm in his and led her to first secret room that they had found. Eilene followed them through the trap door and entered the darkened room. She peered into the atmosphere but there were no images formed.

"But we saw that burning plume right in front of our eyes, dancing around like a little ghost," Geraldo insisted.

"I believe you," Eilene said, thoughtfully staring into the space above her. "Think of something Geraldo. Think of something that has been bothering you."

Immediately, Geraldo's thought manifested overhead. They observed a holographic picture of Arcas emerging victorious on a horse.

"That's what I was thinking," the two dumbstruck Black knights echoed.

"That thought form is a message from your soul. This picture of Arcas in victory is a reflection of yourself that can help guide you."

The sound of thunder pounding outside the castle interrupted them. The thought form immediately disappeared, and so did the holographic image in the room.

"Sounds like the castle is being attacked," Geraldo decided. "Time to go."

The three knights hurried out of the secret room and raced to the highest turret in the castle. In the distance they saw an army of giant metal robots heading straight for them. The weapons were from past galactic wars. Someone else had been editing the Time Line again. Without wasting any time to think it over, Villanti immediately lifted his palms to the sky, drawing in dark storm clouds over the field of shiny metal robots. The rains came and poured on the land as Villanti stayed outside and directed the downpour. The other two drenched knights sought refuge inside the castle, while the metal robots slipped on the wet, grassy field and fell over. This stopped the advancing attack for two days until the robots found traction.

While the other castle inhabitants brought food and blankets to Villanti in the rain, Geraldo left Eilene and returned to one of the secret rooms. He feared for his life, and his thought forms paraded in the air in front of him. He caught a glimpse of his own destruction on the castle towers. Horrified, he raced out of the room and watched Villanti driving the rain toward the metal objects, which had toppled over on the slippery field. Galactic weapons had been developed for outerspace and could not withstand the earth's weather.

Geraldo observed Villanti bring in sunbreaks with his palms. By the end of the afternoon, the machines showed signs of rust. The metal creaked and groaned when directed to move. Satisfied with Villanti's progress, Geraldo walked back to the room where he had previewed his death and contacted his wife and family in Italy. The hologram rooms also communicated with the network of ley lines at the new site near Stonehenge. He reached the portal in the little theater in the middle of Cerchio, Italy and prepared his family for his demise. Then he left the room to join Villanti on the turret.

Igraine met Geraldo just as he was exiting the secret room. "Gamaliel sent me a communication through the portal connection in a secret room. Somebody killed Arcas after the exploding plume in the sky. Maury is dead also, but so is the bishop and his army." Geraldo looked as though he was about to faint, but Igraine's words brought him back to his senses. "I have a mission for you. Go find Maury's surviving daughter, who is here in the castle. She is now Queen of England and those associated with the emperor will want to kill her. She is in grave danger and so is her entire English royal family."

Geraldo nodded. His face regained color and he searched in his mind about where he might find Maury's daughter in the castle. Once he had found an inspiration, he smiled at Igraine and turned down the hallway. With Arcas and Maury gone, he could understand why he and Villanti had stumbled across the secret rooms. Synchronicity happened this way in Camelon, with only a few coincidences. He and Villanti inherited care of the Marlboro connection to the new shataquah around Stonehenge.

Finding Maury's daughter in the room adjacent Tristan's old room, he ushered her down the hall. "You must come with me," he told her. "There will be another attack on the castle soon. I know where you will be safe."

The other six women in the room followed Maury's daughter when she left the room. Some cried hysterically, but the new queen ignored them and focused on the Black knight. He led them down several halls to a series of secret rooms. Something about going past the door to Tristan's former suite soothed Geraldo's fears. They had all spiritually died in prison during the first month. Pellinor had altered the time line and manipulated the weavers of the time line to shorten the life threads of all the knights. The thought of being able to cheat fate had not occurred to Geraldo. In its place, he found a calm acceptance of his destiny. *"C'est la vie,"* he quietly whispered as the French words of Tristan filled his head.

Continuing down his course through the castle, Villanti directed the group of women to the series of secret rooms under the castle. "This room is for your entourage," he said, pushing the frightened women inside and shutting the door. Then he ushered Maury's daughter into the next room and whispered in her ear, "Don't worry about them. This room connects to the first room. When you are ready, you can entertain them. This room is a special room for the new queen of England."

Geraldo silently bowed, leaving her standing perplexed in the middle of the room. Then he closed the door to the room and sealed the secret rooms so that no enemy would ever find them. Information from the portal connection would fill in the gaps in the new queen's understanding. Being a celestial like her mother, she could step into her power when the moment arose.

Geraldo walked upstairs to the highest level of the castle where he helped the rest of the knights defend the castle. The rusted machines had resorted to firing their ammunition from the field. Most of the grenades fell short of the castle, but one exploded near Geraldo's feet on one of the highest turrets. Hitting his head on the stones as the shrapnel tore his gut, he died instantly. His friends took his body through the passageway to the new shataquah, where Laticia retrieved it.

Chapter Twenty-One

EILENE THE GREEN KNIGHT

Giving up material goals
To look for celestial aid
And carry out the mission
For a new life

Tune Reference: *Come Sail Away*

----Styx

IGRAINE MET EILENE in the underground passageway as the horses carried Geraldo's body away from the castle. When she saw Igraine, she dried her tears and waved the horses away. She had been saying her final good-bye to Geraldo before the attendant took the body to the new shataquah. The two women embraced briefly in sorrow, and then Igraine pulled back.

"We need you to bring a message to the Camelon Castle," she told Eilene with a slight smile through her tears. "The communications network through the new shataquah is blocked. Everyone is too grief-stricken to send coherent messages. Horses wait for you in the labyrinth exit for the Camelon road. Whether you are inside or outside the castle, wear a disguise. Tristan's enemies will come looking for you, too. Leave tomorrow; I think that would be best."

"Igraine, I am three months pregnant," Eilene confided. "I believe the child is Tristan's and not the prison guard's. This will be our second. We had a daughter from the autumn fire three years ago."

"Oh! That's the best news I've heard in a long time," Igraine said excitedly. "All the more reason to carry on. Save the bloodlines and keep the love children. The Serpentines are trying to destroy our way of life by infiltrating our DNA, like somebody called Ghengis will do for the eastern world about a thousand years from now. Those civilizations will never be able to regain their spirit."

"It will make future incarnations more difficult. There is a Dark Age descending over the planet," Eilene said with a sigh. "What is the message that that I need to carry?"

"Tell the castle at Camelon that Arcas is dead and that the Castle Marlboro is under siege. The shataquah has been relocated to the Stonehenge area," she replied. Then she explained to Eilene personally, "Laticia's medical services are needed at the new shataquah for the moment. She won't be able to return to Camelon for awhile."

The women departed after another hug and kiss. They paused to listen to hear the explosions from the higher levels of the castle. Eilene chose to spend the night in one of the secret rooms to help gather her thoughts for the mission ahead. Camelon Castle served as a vital communication portal to other global connections. If they missed critical information, then other important areas such as the Druid Island, Wales, and Celtic Lands also were out of the loop.

Entering the same secret room that Geraldo had showed her, she stood in the middle and let her thoughts take shape. Arcas's image appeared in the space in front of her. She sensed that he still inhabited the earth plane and had not yet passed on to the next level. The image seemed very lucid, and she listened for his message.

Without words, he expressed his joy at her pregnancy and urged her to take good care of herself. "Look for two friends along your way," he told her before disappearing as quickly as he had arrived.

Eilene felt a soft warmth and comfort fill the room. Beginning to feel a little drowsy, she reclined in lounge chair near her. Only a desk and afew chairs filled the room. The lighting, like the holographic device, consisted of a combination of mineral and electrical elements. Falling asleep in the darkness, she dreamed that she walked with Tristan in the Flowery Meadows again. They stepped around the flowers as two little girls played near them in the field. Then underneath the flowers, more children appeared until hundreds of boys and girls dotted the Flowery Meadows like white daisies. Tristan turned and kissed her before the dream suddenly ended. The baby within her stirred as she sensed Tristan's breath lingering on her lips. Slowly, Eilene regained her waking consciousness and went outside the room to figure out how much time had elapsed.

In the early morning light, several knights scurryied through the halls to prepare for the more recent attacks on the castle. Eilene refreshed herself as she chose her disguise. Dressing as an elderly man, she cloaked herself and ran to the station at the Camelon exit.

"There you are, Eilene," the elderly woman greeted. She attended the horses at the station. Igraine had already briefed her on Eilene's mission.

"Hello there, Rachel," she smiled with a slight blush. Rachel always saw through her disguises.

"I will always recognize you by your eyes," the older woman fondly told her as she helped Eilene load supplies on the horses. Then she waved as

Eilene rode out of the tunnel and into the light of day. She followed the path through the forest to the Camelon road. Then she galloped away.

Reaching the Camelon Castle by dusk, she reported to Laticia's best friend, who nursed a six-month old infant while several happy toddlers raced around her. Laticia's friend greeted the news with a quiet, sad nod, while preserving the serenity of the children's peaceful world. After relating her message, Eilene left quickly to rejuvenate herself with a walk by the seashore.

Like the dream, she felt that the encounter with the nursing mother had been another glimpse of her future. It represented another life-giving experience that filled her with confidence and determination to survive the present chaos, which threatened to rip their lives apart. Walking slowly along the beach to unwind from her race across the country, she sat down on a nearby log and gazed at the dancing waves in front of her. She spotted the head of a merman in the midst of the white foam. He waved to get her attention. She rose and went out on the pier so that they could talk without his voice being drowned in the waves.

"Go a different route back to the Castle Marlboro. They are looking for someone who is getting messages out of the Castle Marlboro. They sense that energetic information is getting outside of the castle, but they haven't figured out the communications network. It is jamming some of their machines. Luckily they are unable to detect the holographic messages."

Eilene thanked him before departing for her return trip to Marlboro. She recalled that Arcas had told her that she would receive help from two friends. She wondered whether this merman was one of them.

"Look for me in the waves," he told her before he submerged.

Eilene traveled a different road to Marlboro, but felt unsure about how to enter the castle from the forest. No sooner had she begun pondering the problem, then her leprechaun appeared sitting on a giant mushroom to her right.

"Oh, there you are!" she happily greeted him. "I've missed you, my friend."

"Oh yes, there are places where it is no longer safe for us to go," he replied. "I see that you are lost again. Just follow the rainbow to the safest entrance to the castle. Your friend, the merman, will help create one for you."

Then her leprechaun faded away into the forest underbrush. Eilene felt relieved that she had found her safe, magical little world again. However, once she had made it inside the underground labyrinth of the Marlboro Castle, it became a different story. Knights and attendants hurried from passageway to passageway. She heard frequent explosions and falling debris on the upper levels.

Egressa met her in the hallway. "Can you take another message to Camelon?" she whispered in a hushed voice. "We received communication that the Pendragon is on his way to take over Castle Camelon. They must leave quickly."

Eilene gasped. It seemed that Constantinople mounted a world war against all the civilizations in the western Europe. She left Egressa and hurried to the station that Rachel attended.

"Help me with my disguise," she insisted. "One that will fool even you. They are on to me, and I must get through to the Camelon Castle."

Rachel perfected Eilene's disguise before she raced out of the tunnel and into the woods. Dressed as a priest, she returned to Camelon the next morning. Laticia's friend greeted Eilene. The room was filled with toddlers, nursing moms, the recovering Red knight, Maury's partner, and two of Maury's small children.

"Laticia returned late last night," the woman told her. "She is exhausted and still resting."

"You must leave. The Pendragon is coming to take the castle," Eilene told her.

In the room, children wailed and cried as the adults tried to comfort them. Eilene glanced at the many faces around her. Nobody seemed to believe her. Laticia's friend shook her head.

"You must leave now," Eilene repeated.

"Nothing is safer than the Castle Camelon," Maury's partner said as he bounced two small children off his knees.

"I don't see it," Laticia's friend said. "Last I heard the Pendragon remained in Turkey."

Eilene shook her head and gave one last urgent warning, "No, the Castle Marlboro is under heavy attack. The Pendragon is on his way here."

Then she quickly left the Castle Camelon, returning to the Marlboro Castle by the evening. This time Egressa met her in the hallway with another mission.

"Tell them that the Castle Marlboro will fall soon. We can't be expected to last more than a couple more days."

Tears welled in Eilene's eyes when she heard the message. She found a chair in a nearby room and sat down to compose herself.

"Leave when you've had some rest. Don't chance it. We've already lost too much."

Then Egressa left her without any more elaboration.

Eilene rested for the evening and then slipped out of the castle in the early morning light. This time she disguised herself in the cloak of a shepherd. She made it to Antonine Wall before the Pendragon's guards tracked her from the implant she had from prison. In her emotional and pregnant hormonal state, she had failed to see her leprechaun trying to warn her in the forest. She had missed the merman's frantic waves from the river that she had crossed earlier.

Without a warning the Pendragon's guards jumped out of the shadows and sliced her neck. She cried out and then fell motionlessly to the ground. One of the guards raised his sword to cut off her head, but he dropped his sword when he saw a group of Druid priests racing toward them. The attackers fled without laying another hand on her. The Druid priests had seen Eilene running on foot by the wall. They knew that Eilene preferred running to riding and suspected that she brought another vital message. The Druid priests had also watched Pendragon's guards set up the ambush, though they had been too far away to interfere until now. They knelt around Eilene, who still wore her disguise. As they unwrapped the heavy cloak to inspect the wound, they detected her breathes. After quickly stabilizing her, they loaded her on a horse and took her to Laticia.

Eilene regained consciousness and delivered her message directly to Laticia, who had missed the message earlier. Laticia assured her that she would leave the castle immediately with the refugees. She knew how to convince them in their dulled state of denial. As the others packed for the journey, she treated Eilene's wound in another room away from the rest of the castle's inhabitants. Nobody except the Druid priests and Laticia knew that Eilene stayed there. Laticia suspected that Serpentines had placed a tracking device in Eilene's body, so she searched for it during her examination. She found the implant from prison in Eilene's right foot and removed it. Laticia also did a pregnancy check. The developing fetus seemed to be healthy despite Eilene's injury. The heavy cloak had shielded her neck and saved her life. Under the circumstances, Laticia decided to fake Eilene's death and sent her away with the Druid priests until she had fully recovered.

When she removed the implant, she put it in a substitute body, so that the Pendragon forces would think that they had succeeded in killing Eilene the Green Knight.

Chapter Twenty-Two

VILLANTI THE BLACK KNIGHT

There is innovation in craziness
Even solutions

Tune Reference: *You May Be Right*
----Billy Joel

AFTER GERALDO'S DEATH, Villanti remained in his position on the highest level of the castle. He seemed more determined than ever to protect the fortress from the ground attacks He discovered that the rusty galactic weapons could not aim very high. Despite his big, burly frame, he proved as agile as a cat on a high fence. He managed to elude the aim of the galactic weapons and often teased them into misdirecting their fire. Like most machines, it took the mechanical brains awhile to adapt because they were not as flexible as the biological ones.

Between shelling episodes, Villanti would take the underground passageway from Marlboro Castle to the old shataquah site. He focused on dismantling the site to a finer detail than what Dabin could have ever imagine. Then he took over operation of the new shataquah site around Stonehenge, which would have been Arcas's role had he survived. People who understood his talents called Villanti a spell caster because he summoned an incredible amount of elemental energies between his palms as well as directed it coherently. As a result, Villanti added an entire dimension to the Camelon network, taking the operation to a greater level despite the chaotic times.

His forebears had gridded the planet for planetary stability and provided holography for communication. Villanti added elemental balance. This expanded the communication network into harmonic frequencies and secured the planet's position in the universe. Whenever he worked with the harmonics of the new shataquah, he dressed in a manner that incorporated the elemental approach. Otherwise, he wore light pastels. If he wanted to emphasize his connection with the earth, he wore brown colors. Green and yellow represented pollen of opposite genders, where both could be interpreted as either male or female. It didn't matter as long as there was a difference in color for fertilization or creation. Blue represented either the water or sky. Black accepted no other colors, whereas white accepted all. Grays and purples represented a merging. Red stood for fire, which balanced blue or water.

Using these basic combinations, he would sometimes dress completely in one color or half in two different colors. Then he would track who came into the sacred circles of the shataquah for feedback and information. He noted their purpose, their activity, and color of their dress. People who were in harmony wore the same colors, top and bottom. People who wore opposite colors contained each other's energies. For example, one day Villanti wore all blue. Then he tracked who dressed like the earth that day and those who also wore blue. He ignored the rest. This is how he seeded a particular color frequency or dynamic into the system. Days later, he would find someone who came to the shataquah wearing all blue with significant information concerning the water or sky elements.

It wasn't elemental design that made Villanti so popular as a valuable bridge between the various people that served the Camelon network. Not only could he relate to both the land and water spirits well, but he had been born a hermaphrodite. Though his parents never knew what to do with him, everyone else did. In these days, nobody bothered with surgical corrections. These natural enhancements were seen as an asset. He appeared nonthreatening to both genders and could get past communication barriers. Like Egressa, the redheaded Moor, locals viewed him as exotic and he enjoyed popularity at the harvest fires. Also like Egressa, the authorities highly valued him at the castles and he held an important position. Though he had sired a few children, he never became pregnant. When he didn't work as an interpersonal communicator, he chose the masculine and wore light pastels.

As the attacks on the castle intensified, Villanti spent more time dancing around the highest turrets and providing counter fire. Every now and then he successfully knocked out one of the giant robots. Despite his workload, Villanti still found the time to continue his love affair with Maury's daughter, four months pregnant from their romance before the imprisonment. He spent much time in her secret room, where she obtained the information needed for her leadership position. Villanti helped fill in the rest of the details.

One day he decided to check out a secret room on his own. Shortly after Geraldo's death, he entered the secret room that he had discovered with friend. To his surprise, the image of Arcas appeared before him. He thought for sure that Geraldo would manifest in the room to remind him about the money he owed him for a bet on who would die first. Villanti thought that his luck would run out before Geraldo's. He had underestimated his friend's fear of death, which made it occur all that much sooner, because he was too afraid to think his way out of it. Tristan, on the other hand, had forgotten to use caution. Now that many of his close friends had passed on, Villanti saw death differently. Here in the holographic room stood Arcas still exerting his influence despite his passing.

"Aren't you finished yet?" Villanti asked Arcas.

"No," he replied to his friend.

"You seem to have something on your mind," Villanti observed, noticing that the king looked rather stern today.

"So do you," Arcas, quipped, refusing to accept responsibility for Villanti's feelings, too.

Villanti laughed, realizing that Arcas kept him from lapsing into denial. "I am concerned about the knowledge being passed into the wrong hands."

"So am I," Arcas said in a serious voice.

Villanti cocked his head to listen more attentively.

Sensing that he had Villanti's attention, Arcas explained the Black knight's innermost concerns. "Pellinor knows about the underground library. He is under the care of the Mother Superior at the nunnery. She will keep watch on him, but the word is out that we have sacred knowledge. The Pendragon is trying to find it at Camelon."

Villanti took a step back and sat down in the chair next to him. Arcas validated him. Hating the thought of all his work falling into the hands of his enemies, he rubbed his head into his hands for a brief moment and pondered the circumstances. By the time he looked up at the holographic image, Arcas had faded away. He realized that the solution he needed remained within himself.

Leaving the secret room, he went straight to Maury's daughter, who waited for him in her own secret room.

"This is it," she told him.

"You heard..." he replied. They always seemed to be on the same wavelength.

She nodded and kissed him softly on the cheek.

"I'll be around," he said before he left the room.

"I know," she said.

Her words reassured him. He quickly ascended the stairs to the highest turret and resumed the work that he had started earlier. Lifting his arms in the air, he drew the small fire up towards him. The fire roared, and the flames leaped higher and higher in the air around him. He lifted the fire with power in his hands until it engulfed him. He became the fire. It began sweeping through the castle burning every bit of documentation and symbol of knowledge. Nothing escaped its path. Like Villanti, the fire operated very thoroughly and left no record of the Camelon civilization.

Chapter Twenty-Three

LANCELOT THE YELLOW KNIGHT

Strength in perception

Knows when to forgive

And when to live by

One's own rules

And conscience

Tune Reference: *Eye In The Sky*

----Alan Parsons Project

LANCELOT THE YELLOW Knight from France, spent most his time in prison alone. All of his captors seemed afraid of him. He could see right through the bishop, and so the bishop avoided him. He could penetrate whatever miniscule conscience the bishop and guards had left. It made them feel very uncomfortable when they ignored their conscience in Lance's presence. Pellinor, on the other hand, too far gone to listen to his conscience, overlooked Lancelot in the mayhem. Though he had his own cell and plenty to eat and drink, they never released Lancelot because they valued him as a trophy prisoner. He could hear the cries of suffering and agony that occasionally echoed the prison halls, but he remained silent and endured. The other knights could feel his silence and it calmed them with the hope that one lifetime they would have developed immunity from their tormentors.

After Arcas initiated the prison break in the town square, Lance grabbed his son Galahad and they fled the scene. They hid in the forest north of town for several days until the flooding forced them to see higher ground. Then they went to the site of the old shataquah near Avebury. They noticed the scorched ground left by Arcas's battle with the bishop's galactic weapons, and were dumbfounded. It took them awhile to decide what to do next. They didn't trust the security at the Marlboro Castle. They knew that two trumpeters would serve the customer with the biggest purse and decided to go to the Flowery Meadows instead.

Approximately a mile away from the Flowery Meadows, they saw smoke fill the sky and flames dancing over the grasses of the Flowery Meadows. Lance and Galahad turned around and headed for the nunnery on the outskirts of town. They knew that the Mother Superior would welcome them there and offer temporary refuge. However, when they noticed that the town square had also caught fire that afternoon, they changed their minds. Patrols of Roman soldiers roamed the area as the townspeople frantically fought the fire.

Realizing that they had no other alternative, Lance and Galahad decided to deal with the risks at Castle Marlboro, which suddenly seemed the most secure of all their options. They found the new shataquah location around Stonehenge and searched for the tunnel that led to the castle. They wished to avoid the trumpeters, who usually posted themselves in the courtyard. Lance quickly found the passageway, and they headed for the labyrinth underneath the castle. Then they went down several long corridors and climbed the stairs to the southwest turret.

Igraine delightedly greeted them with broad open arms. "You two are a sight for sore eyes. Welcome," she happily said before she hugged and kissed them.

Lance lingered in her embrace momentarily and then returned her affection with a long, passionate kiss as he gently caressed her. Igraine softened and responded to his intimate gesture. Igraine represented another reason why Lancelot had taken a circuitous route. As the couple kissed, Galahad studied the view outside the turret window. His father always deliberated long time before pursuing any romantic relationship. After a moment, Lance and Igraine left the turret for more private quarters.

Egressa entered the room shortly after the couple left. She saw Galahad staring outside the turret window.

"Oh, you're here!" she exclaimed when she met Galahad in the room. "You're just the person I'm looking for."

Galahad smiled slightly and nodded.

"We need an electrician to fix the secret rooms. Villanti's fire threatens the databases, and we need a more secure firewall. Also, the Serpentines are trying to hack the Stonehenge network."

"I'll get on it right away," he said with a smile as he quickly left the room.

"Look Egressa, our new assistant," Igraine announced when Lance accompanied her back into the southwest turret hours later.

"We can always use an extra hand," she replied without looking up from her activity. She never realized the romantic involvement.

"I am sending two knights out to the Camelon Castle to help with the safe passage of the remaining women and children. I expect them any moment."

Within moments, two knights arrived and greeted Egressa, who gave them instructions on the best route for the fleeing refugees. They should be able to pass into the next country safely. It is an international law to provide safe travel for all those who wish to simply travel."

"Oh no problem," one of the knights answered.

"We'll help them with the loading," the other added.

Lance saw through their lies; the two knights worked as negative shape shifters. They would report the refugees to the Pendragon, who discarded international laws. He drew Igraine outside the room and warned her about the knights. Then he left down the hall to warn Galahad, who perceived the world as he did and help him reverse the betrayal.

Igraine returned to the room after the two knights had departed and voiced Lance's suspicions to Egressa without suggesting that the information came from Lance. Egressa ignored her. She seemed preoccupied with something else on her mind. A shudder went up Igraine's spine, but she continued with her work. She deliberated a course, but her emotional shock fogged her thinking processes. The castle began to degrade from within. Eventually, she felt so uncomfortably with her thoughts that she left the room to find Lance.

Unable to locate his son, who worked on the holography in one of the secured secret rooms, Lancelot met Igraine in the hallway as he returned to the southwest turret.

"Egressa has other plans," she told Lance.

"I know. I just saw her leave with the Calepeno out through the magic door. They are abandoning the castle. I saw Calepeno talk to the two trumpeters two hours ago."

"Who is Calepeno?" she asked.

"He is the youngest of the knights. Calepeno abandoned the Avalon outpost about a year ago. He is one of the Black Knights from Italy."

"What about the two knights that Egressa sent to escort Laticia's group?"

"I removed their identification from their bags."

"Are they imposters?" she asked.

"Yes and no. They are shape shifters who play both sides until one side emerges with the clear advantage. Right now their identification papers say that they are officers for the Pendragon. They have already spiritually sold out. Without their identification papers, the Pendragon will kill them along with the rest."

Igraine nodded and softly kissed him on the cheek. She took his arm and together they walked back to the southwest turret. Somebody needed to stay with the castle and protect the network there. In two hours, the armies surrounding the Marlboro Castle broke past the barriers and invaded the castle. They rushed up to the southwest turret and immediately slew the defenders after a brief fight. The fire raged in the corridors outside the room and burned those who crossed its path. Only the bodies of Lance and Igraine remained untouched by the fire.

When the siege had ended, Maury's daughter left the security of her secret room and summoned Gamaliel. The fire slowly died out. The secret rooms and underground labyrinth had been left intact and remained operable. Gammaliel collected the bodies of Lancelot and Igraine from the southwest turret and directed an attendant to take them to the shataquah around Stonehenge. He climbed the stone stairs to the highest turret and recovered Villanti's body. The fire had not touched him either.

Chapter Twenty-Four

GAWAIN THE SILVER KNIGHT

The folly in not being able

To recognize love

Is only redeemed

By having at last discovered it

Tune Reference: *The Search Is Over*

----Survivor

GAWAIN THE SILVER Knight served as King of Scotland, though not a blood relation to either Arcas or Maury. He lived in isolation in the north with several tribes, with a reputation for his pure intentions. On his left hand he wore a diamond ring, which had been in his royal family for generations and worn by each king or queen when they ascended the throne. Despite his reputation for purity, his partner of six years had been captured and sent to the gallows by the bishop on suspicion of witchcraft. Her demise left a widower with three children.

Once word got out that the bishop had imprisoned Arcas, Gawain gathered the surviving knights. Over a million people came to his aid as warriors. Some worked as bowsmen, some became infantry, and some operated as swordsmen. In anticipation that Gawain would rescue the imprisoned knights, Pellinor enchanted the forest around them so that they could not find their way out. Gawain and his army lived too far away to have their fates altered by the weavers of the Time Line. Initially everyone believed that Pellinor had been their ally, so that when he suggested the forest route, Gawain trusted him as did many of the others. They never knew that Pellinor had betrayed them, nor had it occurred to them that they were in an enchanted forest. Convinced that the difficulty arose due to their own lack of skill, they persevered. If they had known that Pellinor had trapped them in a powerful enchantment, they would have relented and moaned their fate.

"Oh, what a cute little bunny," Gawain said as he tried to track his way through the forest. They had been unable to even find past footprints so that they could see where they had been. He watched the bunny disappear in the understory, and leave a series of tracks in the soft mud behind.

"You know, it is almost like someone has been erasing our footprints as we leave them," Gawain remarked to one of his assistants. "The only footprints I've seen today have been the bunny's." Then he shrugged, "I'm taking a break."

Without the notion of foul play ever crossing his mind, he considered his dilemma. He amused himself by playing with the bunny, which had reappeared from the brush. Gawain watched the bunny go underneath a tall tree and hop through the forest in front of the armed warriors.

"Don't kill the bunny," he told the people around him as he dismounted his horse to follow the bunny.

Gawain's command echoed through the vast army trapped in the forest. Gawain forgot his army for a brief moment and became absorbed by the bunny's wanderings, which appeared haphazard to him. Curious, he continued stepping behind the bunny until he could see his way out of the forest. At the edge of the forest, the bunny disappeared in the meadow.

Gawain called to his army to come and find him. By listening to his calls, the army found Gawain and left the enchanted forest.

"Your horse, sire" his assistant said as he handed him the reins to his stead. They had emerged from the forest and gazed at the plains before them.

"Oh yes, thank you," Gawain said politely and almost absentmindedly. His mind dwelled on his next challenge, which consisted of getting through the vast collection of Roman soldiers heading in their direction. Quickly he divided his army into several factions so that they could form a circle around the incoming troops. He hoped to ambush them when they came in closer.

Without raising their weapons, the incoming troops raced towards Gawain. "Why are they waving at us and not raising their swords?" Gawain questioned his assistant as the troops came closer. "Oh my gosh, stop the ambush! It is our own knights, but they are riding Roman horses and using Roman weapons!"

Too late, the divided army slaughtered the knights who had escaped from prison with the stolen the Roman gear. They numbered less than two hundred. Gawain knelt on the ground and sobbed when he realized his mistake. He did not know that Pellinor had already designed the fate of the imprisoned knights. Gawain's army knelt on the ground and cried too. They also had not recognized their own knights in the heat of battle. Then they heard a terrible explosion and observed an enormous burning plume in the sky. The army suddenly quit mourning and rose to their feet.

"I think we need to keep moving forward," Gawain observed as he curiously eyed the spectacle in the sky. "We have had many strange things happened to us today."

Gawain's army pulled itself together and marched forward to Marlboro Castle. Due to their entrapment in the enchanted forest, they had not received updated communication for several days. For various reasons relating to his self-imposed isolation, Gawain remained unfamiliar with the portal system or communications network relating to the shataquahs. His kingdom remained independent from the others, which had preserved its purity at the expense of naivety.

By the time they neared the Castle Marlboro, they stopped. Shocked to see the metal robots closing in on the burning castle, Gawain sat on a log and mourned, "We've missed it again." However, some of the galactic weapons turned around and begin to aim at Gawain's army. "I wonder if this is one of Pellinor's Time Line tricks," Gawain commented to his assistants as he gave the order for army to regroup to the local moors and surrounding mountains.

Then he spied another white bunny hopping around the rusted, but lethal galactic weapons. "Oh look, there's a little bunny," he pointed to his assistants.

"Ah," they echoed together. "A little bunny."

Gawain dismounted and weaved his way down the field towards the bunny. He followed the bunny, which held his own among the giant robots. Too small to be picked up by their sensory devices, the bunny and Gawain eluded the vibration detectors could track the bunny's hops. Eventually one of the machines adjusted its sensors and began to pursue the bunny.

"Don't touch my bunny!" Gawain yelled as he climbed on the offending machine and pierced the sensory device with his sword. Sparks flew from the giant robot and it ceased all motion with a cloud of smoke. The bunny escaped and Gawain leaped after it. He avoided all the other machines as he shielded the bunny from further harm.

"Save the bunny!" several hundred knights cried. They had remained to watch Gawain chase the bunny and desperately wanted to rescue someone or something. Feeling inspired by Gawain's defeat of the giant robot, they ran to the rest of the machines and plunged their swords in the sensory devices. Soon all the rusty machines dropped motionless on the field.

When the smoke had cleared, Gawain led the army towards the castle. The two trumpeters ran out of the castle to herald his arrival. As he neared the castle, several black arrows fell from the sky above them. The invaders inside fired at those who tried to retake the castle. One of the black arrows pierced Gawain's heart and he fell off his horse. His assistants ran to aid him, but the wound proved fatal. He died quietly in their arms moments later.

"It's a black arrow from the league of shadows," the knight observed, after examining the wound. "They fill the world with their pagans, which gives them an excuse for genocide. They work through the bishop's church."

The knight, who held Gawain in his arms, lifted the king from the ground and strapped him to his horse. One of the trumpeters slipped the king's diamond ring off his finger and quickly pocketed it. While the knights took Gawain's body away to Gamaliel on the Druid Isle, the trumpeters took the diamond ring to the associates of the bishop. The bishop's associates paid the trumpeters handsomely for diamond ring. They set the diamond in a jeweled crown, which they intended for a king or queen of their own making.

Chapter Twenty-Five

GALAHAD THE BLUE KNIGHT

It isn't enough to be strong and capable
It isn't enough to survive and endure
Even superman needs a firm hold
For a sure grip on reality

Tune Reference: *Kryptonite*
----Three Doors Down

GALAHAD'S MOTHER HAD been a Dragon flyer from Norway. She met Lancelot while stationed at the base on the Druid Isle. They became fast lovers and remained devoted to each other. During a mission over eastern England, the Pendragon and his Serpentine associates shot her down in midair. They shot down her dragon, too, and both fell to the Earth near present-day London. She died when Galahad was only three years old.

Lancelot mourned the loss of his young wife deeply and sent his son to study with Arcas on Druid Isle. The two boys became good buddies, and Arcas taught Galahad everything he knew about electronics. Galahad excelled at electronics as well as athletics. Being a great team player, he always playing some kind of sport on the Druid Isle. He possessed a gentle spirit and a soft, thoughtful sense of humor. Arcas loved him like a younger brother.

He remained as the electrician at the new shataquah around Stonehenge until the castle fell and communications ceased from the southwest turret. Then he waited for the fire to subside before he checking on the secret rooms, which hid many people from the invaders. Arriving at the castle, he went though many corridors of the underground labyrinth until he found the room that housed Maury's daughter. He ran through the control panel on the outside entrance and released the security lock so that Maury's daughter, Nimue, could reenter the castle.

"It is all over for the moment," he told as she left her room and peered down the hall.

Nimue began sobbing and she hugged him for a long while. He comforted her as she collected herself. Then she went to summon Gamaliel for help. Moved by the woman's emotion, he went into her secret room after she left. He had not visited the southwest turret where he had last heard from his father.

He stood in the middle of Nimue's secret room as his thoughts swirled around him until they finally took shape. The figure of Arcas appeared before him. "I love you," he said.

Galahad smiled slightly with a nod and bowed his head as he sobbed softly.

"We had some good times together," Arcas reminded him. "It only has been rough lately."

Galahad couldn't help but laugh through his tears.

"You know, Galahad, what a superhuman knight like you needs is a room full of roses," Arcas remarked with a slight tease.

Galahad rolled into silent laughter through the tears dripping off his face. Suddenly the room filled with red roses. Their fragrance soothed the Blue knight. His tears ceased.

"I love you," Arcas repeated in a matter-of-fact voice.

Galahad nodded seriously and quit laughing.

"My friends want to you to do something for them," Arcas said with a wink as he faded away. Lancelot and Igraine appeared before Galahad.

Galahad cried when he saw their holographic form. The shock of their appearance reverberated through every bone in his body. An intense grief seized his body and he fell to the ground in sobs. Lancelot and Igraine remained silent as the knight cried and cried. His mother had died when he was too young to cognate her passing. As an older man, he felt a sense of a double loss and finality.

"No!" he wailed.

"Son, get a grip," Lancelot answered.

Igraine quietly nodded, embracing her lover. "Life goes on and so must you."

Galahad raised his head and faced the image of his father and Igraine.

"The two knights escorting Laticia's group are negative shape shifters. Make sure that they get the wrong information," his father instructed, before fading away with these last words.

They are all still fighting, even from the other side, Galahad thought. Then he quickly changed the subject in his mind as the scent of roses overpowered the room. The red roses appeared again and surrounded Galahad until he fell into a gentle sleep on the floor.

Sometime later, the Blue knight awoke in the darkness. "I love you too, Arcas," he murmured in his semiconsciousness. Opening his eyes wide, he immediately rose from the floor and exited the room. He ran through the passageways to the new shataquah to fulfill his father's request.

"Kryptonite," he told his male teammates at the shataquah around Stonehenge.

"Oh yes, kryptonite," one of his fellow electricians whispered.

"Put it in the saddlebags of the horses of the knights going to escort Laticia's group," Galahad told him.

"Will do," his teammates echoed.

Then Galahad quickly left his camaraderie of knights at the shataquah for the underground labyrinth of Marlboro Castle. He spent the rest of the day tending to the electronics protecting the secret rooms. The next afternoon he met Nimue in one of the corridors.

"The Serpentines have figured out how to jam the signals out of the castle," Nimue related. Even though they can't find us, they know that we are still alive here."

Galahad gave her one of his characteristic silent nods.

"The Pendragon ambushed Laticia's group. She saw it coming. She and her daughter survived by hiding in the tall grass by the stream. The negative shape-shifting knights were killed along with the rest. The Pendragon can't track us now, thanks to you."

Galahad smiled quietly at her kind words and then headed for the southwest turret where his father had died. This time he didn't come to mourn. The bodies had already been taken to the Druid Isle. He came to look for clues that might save the new shataquah connections. He rummaged through the desks in the room. Villanti's fire had effectively burned everything. He stopped and looked at the view outside the turret window. Gazing at the early morning sunrise, he realized that he had lived in a timeless void over the past few days and he visually embraced the dawn of a new day. Here he stood in the castle, after having survived the world's darkest hour. Both Gawain's efforts on the field and Villanti's fire had destroyed the enemy and secured his present view outside the turret window. If it had not been for all these efforts, he would not be here now experiencing the rebirth of a new day.

Turning from the view outside the window, he faced the ashes left in the stone room. His father and Igraine no longer operated the Intelligence headquarters, but their spirit still lingered in the room. He could feel their love all around him, like the roses from Arcas's in the secret room. Their love shielded him from the revelation that hit him while he stared at the empty space inside the room. It occurred to him that the Serpentine Federation might try to access the holography in the secret rooms. They might discover the kryptonite in the saddlebags of the knights and use it to alter the projections in the secret rooms. The vulnerability loomed as the weak link in the Camelon network.

He hurried to Nimue's secret room and checked the control panel, which confirmed his worst fears. The kryptonite imprint on the shield protected the room. Geraldo had put the shield in place before he died. Although the imprint could not penetrate the information projected in the room, it could pervert it and cause the inhabitant to go insane.

He ran to his team left at the shataquah and told them the dilemma.

"I need to reverse the imprint," he told them. "If something happens to me, hold onto my original resonance."

His team nodded gravely.

With their heartfelt expressions engrained in his memory, Galahad walked back through the passageway and began to take apart the control panel of Nimue's secret room. Then he crossed a few wires together and reversed the signal. A few lights flickered on the panel, assuring him that he had been successful. However, he had not detected that the apparatus had been booby-trapped. The sword proved to be double-edged. Although the reversed signal would destroy the nest of Serpentines on the other end, the counter shock would kill anyone who tampered with the nest.

Several amps jolted Galahad as he closed the lid of the box. He could not let go. The electrical intensity increased and electrocuted him.

His teammates at the new shataquah knew immediately that the system had become overloaded. They sent some knights to disconnect Galahad from the shock, but it proved futile. His limp body fell to the ground when the circuit breaker responded. Meanwhile they held his original resonant frequency, which had manifested in the middle of the new shataquah.

"Good-bye. I love you," his holographic image said before fading away.

Chapter Twenty-Six

Live your dreams

And overlook the odds

The dead are the ones

Who never allowed themselves

To be carried away

By the currents of desire

Tune Reference: *Wasted On The Way*

----Crosby, Stills, and Nash

GAMALIEL COLLECTED THE bodies of Arcas and the twelve knights and placed them on separate funeral pyres. These twelve knights served the inner circle of the Round Table, and each knight played a significant role in the history of Camelon. After escaping the ambush on the field, Laticia helped with preparations and found a substitute body in place of Eilene's. Eilene attended her own funeral disguised as an old man, one of her more successful costumes. Only the Druids that accompanied her could see through her disguise. They helped her light Tristan's pyre before it sailed downriver. Then she helped Laticia light Arcas's pyre. Two of her children on the Druid Isle had been the result of past harvest celebrations with Arcas. They had spent three Druid Fires together, and she had raised the boy and the girl in secret. Arcas never suspected and only Tristan knew about the children. Although they knew that Arcas would be furious at them for keeping this secret, they wanted to protect the identity of the children. She could tell them once they had survived to adulthood. The children remained on the Druid Island to help raise the Furry dragon nestlings just as Arcas had done in his youth. The pyres were lit at the Druid Isle and sent down river to the scorched fields of the Flowery Meadows. People from many countries lined the banks of the river and threw red roses at the burning pyres as they floated downstream.

Arcas remained on the earth plane for the life celebration. Laticia could feel his presence hovering near her as she danced around the burning pyres. Recalling the Shiva dance of life and death, Laticia mourned her lover, her sister, and her best friend. As seven months pregnant, she no longer could conceal the pregnancy, though people never noticed in their state of shock. She hid in the shadows around the central bonfire and danced in the shower of red rose petals that fell all around her. She sensed Arcas dancing with her, recalling the delight shining in his eyes like the stars twinkling in sky.

A light mist veiled the celebration from the eyes of their enemies. It remained light enough to provide visibility from the stars, but enough to shield them from intruders. The merpeople swam in the river with a soft luminescence emanating from their bodies in the dark. Fireflies swirled in the air, casting off streaks of soft blue and green light. Here in the midst of grief and destruction, the magic of the natural world shone brilliantly. This comforted those who had gathered for the life celebration.

The Thunder People made their presence known by lighting the haze with bolts of lightning and an occasional rumble of thunder. All the knights, including Eilene had been so badly traumatized that they had gone to another dimension to protect their souls. With them went the soul of the Camelon network. The survivors would infiltrate the new regimes until the time came for the souls to be retrieved from the other dimension. They held the space for the return of Arcas and the Camelon knights, the *promise of Camelon*. Laticia and the others who understood this could see the dimension projected holographically over the waters as the pyres burned downstream. The image of an airship could be seen rising above the burning pyres. This is where the souls of the knights had gone for safety. Their enemies could not reach them in this other dimension.

The funeral pyres drifted downriver and disappeared in the waters around the Flowery Meadows. The Flowery Meadows remained vacant until a grove of fireweed healed the land. Then the flowers returned, and wild red roses dotted the countryside. No human inhabited the place for another two hundred years.

Laticia danced through the night until the dawn of a new day. Still wearing her disguise, Eilene came and sat down beside her on the beach. She watched Laticia gaze at the river, which was placid compared to the previous night. The woman seemed lost in another world and did not acknowledge Eilene's presence.

Eilene interrupted the silence between them. "Do you recognize me?"

"Yes." Laticia smiled still focusing on the light mist circling over the river. "You helped me light Arcas's pyre. Your own pyre is floating down the river."

"That is all I need to know," Eilene replied.

"There is something I need to know," she told Eilene.

"Well, you probably know it then," Eilene answered.

"Fair enough," she said. "Two of the children caring for the nestlings resemble Arcas in manner and in appearance. Gamaliel showed me one day while we collected the dead. You had them before he even knew I existed."

Eilene whispered, "I felt that I only had him for a moment."

"Same here," Laticia echoed softly. "One brief shining moment, like Camelon itself."

"At least we had it," Gamaliel said as he wondered near the two women. "Past civilizations have been fighting for a very long time, but none of them ever flourished. They just survived but never really thrived. That is what we get to keep and carry on through lifetimes. The emotional joy that we found in our lives will light our souls forever."

"That is how we won the war," Laticia commented. "Though the battle continues."

Laticia stood, revealing her pregnant form. She wandered to the river a few yards away and waded in the gentle waves.

Eilene felt a shock wave go through her body at revelation of Laticia's pregnancy and she feared for the woman's life. There were many who would kill her to stop Arcas's bloodline.

"I plan to return home to my village and raise my daughter. It is the only life I know and I will follow this path to the end."

"Your village belongs to the Pendragon now," Gamaliel reminded her.

"I know, and he thinks the new baby is his," Laticia said as she stared into the mists again.

Remembering her encounters with the prison guard, Eilene shuddered at Laticia's poignant announcement. Tears welled in Gamaliel's eyes.

Laticia continued with a hint of chagrin in her voice, "The bishop's associates gave the Pendragon a crown for his heir. It has Gawain's yellow topaz set in it." Turning around to face Eilene, she requested, "Promise me that if anything should happen to me that you will allow the Pendragon to make this baby the next king as if it is his own son. You will know him by his name, Arthur. I suspect that the Pendragon is sterile and Arthur will be his only heir. The man is desperate and has already sold his soul."

Both Eilene and Gamaliel looked at each other in disbelief and then nodded.

"Thank you for keeping my secret," said Laticia said. "I must go now and slip back into the village before they realize I am gone. I am also a master of disguises," she concluded, winking at Eilene.

Gamaliel kissed her softly on the cheek and waved her off. Laticia left the beach and disappeared into the forest.

"Shall I escort you back to your Druid bodyguards?" Gamaliel asked as he helped Eilene to her feet. Then he solemnly changed the subject. "If anything should happen to me, then the care of the Merwyns will fall to you. There is no one left who knows the lore as well as the traditions. The Serpentines will seek me out now that the castles have fallen. I am the decoy for the new shatquah around Stonehenge."

"Please take me back now," Eilene said softly. "I have work to do."

"Don't forget to take time out to smell the roses," Gamaliel reminded her as he took her arm in his and walked back towards the Druid village on the island.

Leaving Eilene at her new home, he went back to his stone cottage. Eilene watched Gamaliel fade into the early morning sun and then tended her hearth. A man walked in the room carrying an armful of wood and set it before the fire. Afterwards, he walked over to her and kissed her on the cheek. She touched his arm and responded with a long deep kiss. Feeling the dawn of a new day stirring within her, she planted the sensation firmly on his lips. Aroused, he caressed her hair and face. She met his fervor as he lifted her into his arms. Then he carried her to the little bed in the corner of the room.

Later that morning the couple rose from the bed and enjoyed a late breakfast before going to instruct the children who cared for the nestlings. When they reached the nest, a group of small children greeted them. Eilene realized that the majority of the children resembled Gamaliel. Many of the Druid women wanted his baby, and he satisfied them. He had many children of his own as well as those who he had adopted.

"Tell me how the leprechauns find their pot of gold?" one little boy asked. He favored Arcas and wiggled into Eilene's lap as he wrapped himself in her arms.

"With their minds," she told him as she glanced down at the boy snuggling against her body. "Then it just appears in front of them."

"You must look for the rainbow," Eilene's lover added, sitting down beside her on the bench. He held two children in his arms. "Follow the person who pursues the dream."

Epilogue

Egressa and Calepeno the Black Knight abandoned Marlboro Castle through the magic door, a portal to present-day Austria. After wandering through the mountains for half a year, they parted ways. Later, the Turks captured Calepeno and inducted him into the local army. Being very talented, he quickly rose through the ranks to a leadership position. Hundreds of regimens came under his control, though only fourteen years old at the time. Eventually breaking under the strain of command, he maintained isolation from the home that he had enjoyed with the Camelon network. He entertained the delusion that he represented the only survivor left to carry out the Camelon mission, which conflicted with his present position. As a result, Calepeno became a megalomaniac. As his enormous army grew and grew, he went on a killing spree destroying anyone who opposed him. When Constantinople realized that they had created a monster, they sent out several armies to kill Calepeno. Their success at a high cost.

Some of the Druids became high-ranking members of the clergy and sought reforms within the system. Though, it took a thousand years, Constantinople fell through infiltration. Michael, the altar boy who had assisted Maury the Silver Knight, rose through the hierarchy and became Bishop of Canterbury after a year. Later he went on to be Cardinal while continuing to run interference in support of the Camelon survivors.

Meanwhile, the armies associated with Morgaine Le Fey turned on each other. They blamed each other for the mistakes made during the warfare with the Camelon network. After the death of Mordred, the armies lost their confidence and their drive. They decided that they no longer wanted to spend their lives destroying leprechauns, fairies, and Merwyns. The earth spirits were getting harder to find. Instead, they opted for the easier target, which happened to be Morgaine Le Fey. The troops mutinied at sea, and the captains banded together against Morgaine Le Fey. They marched on her castle and killed her before she could retaliate.

Back at the Camelon village, Laticia delivered a healthy boy, whom she called Arthur. She had already given her daughter up for adoption in the royal network surrounding the Pendragon. He never learned of Arcas's daughter, who survived and eventually made her way to the refugees in Wales. She studied with the son of Egressa and Merilyn there and lived a long life. The Pendragon continued to believe that he had fathered Laticia's son. Two months after delivering the baby, Laticia died in her sleep after ingesting a weed that she knew would kill her. This secured the identity of the child, and no one could question her.